Remarkably Great

For Caroline,
Have a remarkably great escape!
Best wishes,
Heather

Remarkably Great

By Heather Grace Stewart

Graceful Publications

Edited by Jennifer Bogart

ISBN: 978-0-9918795-3-3

Also by this author

Strangely, Incredibly Good

The Friends I've Never Met (digital screenplay)

Three Spaces

Carry On Dancing

The Groovy Granny (Kindle, Kobo; audio version on iBooks)

Leap

Where the Butterflies Go

More info: www.heathergracestewart.me

All Books: www.author.to/hgracestewart

For Larry,
I miss you asking for 'More pages! More pages!"
Every single day.
But I keep them coming,
In your memory.
See you at the movies.
For G.G.,
For being remarkably great, and for
spiking the punch bowl
at the senior's residence
and telling me about it. ☺

Chapter One

Tuesday, February 14, 2017

"Here, let me get that for you." Will opens the restaurant door and gestures for me to go ahead inside.

Hmm. Nice. Chivalrous. Old school. And he smells so good! Modern, musky. CK One, maybe, mixed with a manly soap? He uses soap. Hallelujah! Maybe I need to have a better attitude about this. Maybe this date will be different.

It's my second date this month. I'd promised myself, as

well as my feisty 94-year-old Gram, that I'd try to forget Gene, my beloved Genie MIA, and try dating again.

As soon as we enter the Italian restaurant, a bald man with bulging eyes, a tight red vest, and a creepy smile makes love to me with his accordion. Going out on a blind date on Valentine's Day wasn't one of my wiser decisions. Still, I'll give this Will a chance. It's not his fault the restaurant owner hired a horny accordionist and put kissing penguins at every table. I feel like I'm in a Disney film.

Love. What is true love, anyway? Gram keeps reminding me true love waits, but it also gets back to you quicker than three and a half years. "Hell. Even Fed Ex does better than that," she says.

I defend Gene all the time. What if he's stuck in stasis in an old lamp, or with a terrible master who won't let him contact me? He'd never leave me like this if he could at all help it. He loves me.

Besides, he sent me that beautiful bouquet, with its hint of wonderful things to come. It's all he could do at the time; I know he's coming back for me. So, I figure I'll appease Gram and my older sis, Cici, who tells me, "You can't give up on love at forty-one," and get a few free dinners at the same time.

I miss laughing with Gene. He had (has? I don't want to imagine the worst; I cannot conceive of him no longer existing) the most contagious chuckle! I always thought I'd hear it again.

You take the smallest things for granted when you love someone. The way their eyes crinkle at the corners when they laugh. The way they place their head on their pillow. The way they sip their coffee, lick their ice cream, put on their shoes. Those things are unique to every person. I like to watch and compare closely. It's a beautiful art form called personality. Sadly, I only realized this once Gene disappeared. After he was gone, I realized how much I missed the way he used one foot to squish down the heel on his sneaker so he could place the other foot inside without bending down. It used to annoy the hell out of me. Why couldn't he put his shoes on like normal people? Why? Why be so lazy?

I'd give anything to have my not-normal guy back again. I know that quirks make a person who they are, and when you truly love someone, you love the whole package. You love all their flaws and eccentricities.

Will is drumming his fingers on the table, glaring at me.

"Oh, I'm so sorry, I was lost in thought." I sip my wine and flash him a warm smile, hoping he'll forgive me for staring into space. I need to stop thinking about Gene! I'm on a date, here! I'm moving on! Moving on!

"Supposably you want to be here?" he says, still looking irritated. "I have other matters to attend to, tonight." He fiddles with his thin green tie. "Matters of upmost importance."

Oh, my! That was rude, and incorrect! Maybe he's a little heavy-handed on the red wine. He's slurring his words. Maybe that's what made him say supposably and upmost. Don't be a snob, Cat. Let it slide.

"Yes, of course, I want to be here. Look around us! The mood is set for romance!" I try my best to sound chipper, despite the 20-something in the corner sitting on her boyfriend's lap. It looks like her tongue has a mind all its own. It's trying to have sex with his ear.

I look away and stare down at my empty plate. I wish the waiter would bring us some bread. After all Gene did for me, helping me lose the extra weight I was carrying, letting me forgive myself by changing traumatic events in my past, I could shoot myself for letting the weight creep up again this winter. I'm not as big as I was before, thanks to the twice-weekly workouts at the gym I own and manage, The Cat Walk, but I'm not uber-fit, either. There's still that persistent muffin top.

I have too much paperwork lately because of our plans for expansion this summer. Most days, I find myself munching on M&M's at my desk while peering out at the tanned and toned bodies fifteen feet away on the elliptical machines. I know I have to curb the snacking (or possibly close my office door), but a part of me is beginning to believe that weight around the belly is a frightening, unwelcome gift that arrives at your door at 40. It's a gift you don't want, but can never, ever return. I shudder. Bah! My belly is a cheap horror movie.

It's not just how I feel about my weight that makes me shaky. It's Valentine's Day, and Wrong Word Will is making me nervous. I'm craving the carbs! Bring me my bread! Maybe if I make small talk, I'll forget about it.

"So, Will, tell me about your latest case. I've never dated a scientist, before. What line are you in?"

"I study humans. Cadavers, actually, and how they decompose."

My wine goes down the wrong way. I'm sputtering so much I think I stained my crisp white blouse. Grabbing a napkin, I stuff it in my mouth to stop the flow. Breathe, Cat, breathe. It could be worse. He could cook Meth, too. You could be dating the guy from Breaking Bad. A few more breaths, and you'll be able to speak again.

"How fascinating. What do you do with your, er, findings?" I try to recover with an overzealous grin.

"Pacifically, I'm the top embalmist in Ottawa. When your famous Gram finally kicks the bucket, you should come see me." He laughs at his own joke, but then I notice he's putting his card on the table.

Pacifically? I'm not sure what offends me more: that he preserves dead bodies, that he wants to preserve my Gram, or that he can't speak English.

"Thanks, Will, but I'm pretty sure she's going to outlive us all."

"Hey, I was wondering if after this... if you wanted... after this..."

Now Will can't get his words out. Oh come on, just spit it out! Why's he hesitating? Maybe it's something sexual?

"Wanna go see decomposing bodies?"

I choke on my wine again, but this time, I let it dribble out of my mouth and down my chin. Whatever! I'm not the ridiculous one, here! I heard him, but I can't believe what I heard. Am I being punked? I look around for cameras. Nope. Not one. This is insane! I'm stuck inside a trending Twitter stream. Hashtag: Worstdatein5words. I won't answer. I've lost my will to speak, anyway.

Our pasta has arrived, and, thank God, the bread! I grab a soft, warm bun and devour it like a lioness eating its prey. I don't care that I've been teased about my eating habits in the past. I don't care about the calories, and I certainly don't care about looking ladylike. Not tonight. My goal is simply to survive this ridiculous date.

Accordion Man's at our table. Of course. He's flirting with my plate of pasta. The tune sounds like a sad funeral march, and it reminds me of what Will does for a living. I don't think I can stomach the rest of my meal.

"About your Gram," Will continues. I thought he'd dropped that subject. No such luck. "You should make sure she's written a will. You may think she has, but you never really know. By all intensive porpoises, a will is legally binding."

"What did you just say?" Porpoises? I'm laughing so hard tears are streaming from the corners of my eyes. It's an odd feeling, to get such delight out of his errors, because he's messing with my family, too. I can feel my blood pressure rising even as I continue laughing out loud.

"Try to follow me here, Cat. I know you're just a lowly gym rat," he sneers. "I said—"

"That's it." I stand up, throwing my napkin down on my plate. "You're not only rude, you not only think you're superior, but you're also just plain wrong. My Gram is none of your business, and you need to Google all those fancy expressions you think you're using correctly."

I grab my purse and head for the door, think better of it, and turn on my heels. I walk back to the table, take his plate with my free hand, and dump his meal on his head. Linguine noodles are sliding off his hair and down his face in a tiny tornado of tomato sauce, capers and cheese.

"That's for calling me a gym rat."

"Don't stop believin', hold onto that feelin'..." Journey's classic song fills the car as I sit here, head in my hands, wondering where to go next.

In life. I mean, in life.

How did I get to this place again, where I'm dating losers and aching for one of those Deep 'N Delicious chocolate cakes right out of the plastic pan? Tears start streaming down my face, and I'm not even wearing my new waterproof mascara. Fuckity! My life is a travesty!

I'm thankful I drove to meet Will in my own car, but so angry I believed I could find someone like Gene. There's no one else out there for me. It's not like I believe there's only one person for everyone, and that we all have soul mates picked out for us at birth. That's a load of crap that belongs out back with your Lhasa Apso. But when you meet someone who 'gets you', who lets you be yourself while helping to create a better version of you, that's damn difficult to replace. I feel like I'm not truly living without Gene. I'm going through the motions. It's like everything is grey, right down to my tattered underwear. That's because I had to have this $65 grey bra and panty set in La Senza when I saw a sign saying, "Grey. It's the New Black."

But, no. It's not the new black; it's just grey, and it fell apart in the washer, leaving me with a set of shitty undies, and a bad case of shopper's remorse.

Enough. I need to stop moping around and do something about this. The only way to get the color back in my life is to find Gene.

So, where, or possibly, when, the hell is he?

Chapter Two

Saturday, February 18, 2017

Are you disciplined enough, Cat Glamour?

No! Not again. It's my earworm from that album called High School Hell. Why does my mind always go back there when I'm working out? It's so weird.

I try to push the memories out of my mind as fast as possible. Concentrate on the now, Cat. Focus on the now. You still have 25 sit ups to do.

I attempt to lay back on the gym mat and focus on my client, Trina, and the songs playing on the Cat Walk speakers. It's no use. I can't stop these incessant thoughts. The dreadful, horrible memories keep flooding in, along with the sweat on my brow.

"Are you disciplined enough, Cat Glamour?"

Cathy Hollow's deep brown eyes met mine with a condescending glare as she placed an Aero Bar in front of me on my cafeteria tray. I looked up slowly and locked eyes with her, prepared to play her game. I would be brave. I would resist.

My stomach must have thought that it was jumping vault, but I couldn't let any of them see my anxiety. They knew I was dieting. They'd seen me eating a salad with Ben earlier, and every day this week. This was payback time. They didn't want any eligible boys hanging out with me. I was the fat girl, and by approaching me, they had hung me high like a dartboard, for all to see.

They'd throw darts at me for the rest of my high school years.

"Sure, I'm disciplined," I tried to control my voice so I sounded unscathed. "More than you are when you study. What did you get on last year's History exam, again? Oh right, you slept in and missed it. Now, that's discipline."

"Don't talk back to me, fat ass." That was enough to send Cathy's posse, three other grade ten girls who were brunette clones of each other, into a fit of giggles.

"Yeah, Fat Cat," Moira, the tallest of the bunch, added

as she unwrapped the foil on the chocolate bar and waved it under the bottom of my nose, giving me a good long whiff of that sweet cocoa smell.

"Put it down in front of her, Moira." Cathy had everyone in her group on a tight chain. "Let's leave Fat Cat to devour it alone. Save her the embarrassment of us top lionesses staring her down while she eats her prey."

"You are disciplined, and you've come such a long way. Way to go, girl!"

I stand up, wipe my forehead with my towel, give Trina a high five, and check off that she'd completed today's Cat Walk workout on my clipboard. As I look down, I catch a glimpse of myself in the floor-to-ceiling mirrors beside the weights. I'm 5'4", but my legs look longer and more slender in these purple Lululemons. I must make a mental note about that. My new blonde bob doesn't hide the wrinkles around my blue-grey eyes, and I still can't find a concealer that adequately disguises those dark blue circles. God, I look tired. I've been working too many late nights, lately. Alone, naturally.

"You are such an inspiration to me, Coach Cat. You've sure convinced me that life begins at forty!" Trina laughs.

"You have no idea." I chuckle. If she only knew that for me, it was more like I was reborn at 38, nearly four years ago. That's when I got a whole new life, and a much slimmer body, in the most strange and incredible way.

"Thanks for the motivation. I'm not going to thank you for all those squats, but..." Trina gives me a sweaty hug. I hate sweaty hugs, but it's a good feeling to know I've made a difference in her life.

I sit down on one of the red benches along the wall, hold out her water bottle, and motion for her to sit with me.

"That's okay, Coach Cat," Trina takes her water bottle and grabs her towel. "I need to hit the showers. I'm late for taking Zac to his friend's birthday party," she says. "But thanks for another great workout, and for motivating me so well all week."

"Anytime. You're doing great." Coach Cat. I'm still not used to hearing that. What a transition from Fat Cat. I don't even need to say, 'if only Cathy and Moira could see me now', because, they have seen me.

In fact, they're over with Justine in one of the exercise rooms, taking their weekly Zumba class. Moira has even asked if I'd be free to take her on as her trainer. I looked at my schedule briefly, and then said, "Sorry, there's too long a waiting list," without any hesitation, making sure Cathy overheard every word. Damn, that felt great.

I walk into my office and plunk myself down in my red leather chair. It's closing time soon, thank goodness. I'm really stiff and can't imagine training one more person today. As I begin to tidy a few pens and papers on my desk, I accidentally knock over my desk calendar, and it flips to May. My heart skips a beat, and I can't help staring at one particular day: May 4th 2017.

I have so much riding on that date. I don't want to live my life waiting for that day, but if it means what I think it means... if it's my only chance to be reunited with my Gene... Oh God. I so want to hold onto hope; to hold onto it like you'd hold onto a Gucci purse in the New York subway. I'm afraid, though, that I've been letting go of hope, and my dreams, a little more with every passing year.

I blink back the tears and try to compose myself by looking through the wide windows to Exercise Room 2. Moira and Cathy look like they are struggling to get the Zumba moves right. Moira is tripping over Cathy's left foot, and Cathy's trying to recover by shaking her behind. She looks like a 40-year-old, dehydrated penguin. Twerking. Meanwhile, the rest of the class is doing an actual Zumba move. Cathy is completely lost.

I look closer. She actually looks tired, like me. Human. Imperfect. I wonder why I ever cowered around her. She's as messed up as any of us.

Funny. We're all winging it while pretending that we're not. The ones who say otherwise are better liars. So few of us women admit it. I wonder why that is?

I'm winging this being thin thing. I don't know how long it'll last, but I act confident. Hell, I even own a gym. Cathy and Moira have no idea I sometimes lie awake in bed, worrying about gaining all the weight back. They have no clue I feel like a phony, like I don't have the discipline I need to keep the extra pounds off. To them, I'm their high school's greatest success story: the one who realized she was married to a deadbeat, left him, and worked hard to follow her dreams and build her own business.

If they only knew about Gene. I imagine us weight-lifting together:

"You turned your life around. You're just such an inspiration to me, Cat," Cathy would say after a few lifts of the 10-pound dumbbells.

I'd smile and answer with confidence. "Well, I did have a little help from this magical genie dude who popped out of my Wii. Then, we fell in love and had steamy sex in a French castle." She'd probably drop the dumb bells on her feet.

When I think about the strange, incredibly good events of the past few years, I wish I believed it were all a dream. That'd be so much easier to explain to people. You can't casually drop into a conversation over beer and nachos with friends and mention you had a modern day genie magically appear from out of your Wii machine. I haven't been able to explain to anyone other than my Gram that Gene helped me get my life back on track when I needed him most, but then disappeared to save my life. Some days I have a hard time believing it happened myself, but despite that nearly four years have passed, I still believe in him. I still believe in us.

No, they can't find out. No one but Gram can know my little secret. I work hard every day to keep the weight off, to run this gym efficiently. It's not like I'm a complete phony. Everyone knows I had a minor heart attack a few years back. I try to change the topic when that comes up, because I hate feeling weak. Still, no one knows that magic got me where I am today, and no one can ever find out.

Knock-knock. Justine's at my door. "You almost done here, Cat?"

I hadn't even noticed our background music had stopped. "Go ahead. I have lots of paperwork to catch up on. I'll lock up."

"Sure," Justine says, "but it's Saturday night, Cat, so don't work too hard." She heads for the main door.

Make yourself look busy. That's my second secret, and it's almost as big as the one about the genie. Never let them see you slack. Then, no one can ever call you a fat phony.

Chapter Three

Brrrr. My condo's cold. I close my door, kick off my boots, hang up my coat, and drop my keys on the hall table. I'll put on a fire and read that novel I've been wanting to start. I'll have a sophisticated night alone with a glass of red wine. What's wrong with that? Nothing. Nothing is wrong with enjoying your own company on a Saturday night.

Except, as I find that last TV dinner in the freezer and pop it in the microwave, I wish I were a better cook. Gene used to tell me he'd cook a gourmet, four-course meal for me. We never got to enjoy any of that. We had such a short time together. Blissful, but far too short.

I have to stop thinking about him! This could torment me for life! Okay, tonight I will not think about men. No. More. Man. Thoughts.

I pour myself some wine, sit down on the couch, turn on the TV, and check out the guide. Let's see. It looks like my choices are: "Mormon Half Love" or "The Man With the 132 lb Scrotum."

Seriously? This is my Saturday Night? There is not enough wine in this house for me to even contemplate watching these shows. And yet... this is definitely better than dating.

Oh, look, it gets better. Later tonight, on TLC, we have "The Girl With Half a Face", "The Man Who Lost His Face", "The Man with Half a Body", and "The Man with the 200 lb Tumor."

Fuckity. If only I could have my Man Who Grants Wishes In A Whirl of Purple Smoke. He's all I want!

I turn off the TV and pick up my tablet from the coffee table. Maybe Gram has posted some new Tweets that will entertain me. She often does.

I go to her @BadAssGrandma timeline and find my frown turning into a grin as I read her latest tweets.

<Don't get this fascination with Vampires. You wanna hang out with pasty faced men that sleep all day? Get married. You'll see.>

<Follow me, don't follow me, I don't give a rat's ass. I'm 94 years old, for God's sake. I won't remember where my I put my panties tomorrow.>

<Sometimes I pretend I forget where I live, just to mess with people. Amazing how much Starbucks an old lady can get with that one.>

I laugh out loud at the last one. Yup, those are definite winners. I'll have to tell her I liked those when I see her next.

I'm not much of a retweeter, and I never 'like' items. Online, I'm more of a lurker; I prefer face to face conversations.

As I scroll down my timeline, my eyes are inundated with digital graffiti. Mostly, Twitter is full of lonely people advertising their balls, their books, or their boobs. There are, however, a few fascinating people I like to follow. I scroll further and notice a photo of a pink tube of cream. What's that? 18 Again? You've got to be kidding me. Vaginal Shrink Cream exists, and someone's advertising it on here? Saying women over 40 need tighter vajayjays to attract men? I am seriously disturbed by this. Geeeezus! Sometimes I want to log off of society.

Too bad you can't actually log off of society. Well, you can, if you go find yourself a deserted island and live there without satellite or wifi. If I did, what would my luxury item be? Hmmmm. A razor? Nope. No one around worth shaving for. Hair dye? Definitely not, who cares about grey roots when you're all alone and there are no mirrors? Gosh, I'm liking this island idea more and more. I wouldn't even have to worry whether thick eyebrows are in or out! Not that I do, but it's on every freaking magazine cover, lately. Right now, they're in.

Live on a deserted island. I must remember to jot this down in my Ideas Journal. Maybe Gene can take me to live with him on an island someday. Maybe in the future you're gonna come back... gonna... damn you Sara Bareilles, you and your perfect songwriting skills. I don't want to cry tonight! I must stop thinking about that song.

I've got it! My luxury item would have to be a lifetime supply of coffee, a cup, bodum, and a kettle. Oops. Can all that count as one luxury item? Oh, whatever. It's my fantasy. Mine! I can make it how I want. Mmmm... the aroma alone would make my lonely island living complete.

What was I doing? Oh right, Twitter, because it's there. That should be their slogan.

Scroll on, Cat. Scroll on. There's got to be something slightly half decent further down! I finally notice a tweet that's been retweeted 100's of times. Okay. It's a link to a blog post. This should be informative! I click and read the title.

Ghosts, Ranked by Hotness

Seriously? I can imagine the banter in the comments' section of the blog: "Oh, Casper has nothing on Patrick Swayze!"

I need to log of the Net. Now.

I put down the tablet, pick up the novel I've been reading, and pour myself another glass of wine. Okay, I'll just read a novel. This is what mature adults do when they're alone. I don't need a man. I don't need to Tweet. I don't need some dance club beat. I'll expand my mind!

I start with the back cover blurb: Monica's marriage has dissolved, and her children have grown up and left home. She takes them to the local fair, hoping to revive what's been lost in their relationship. Once there, a young magician sweeps her off her feet.

Divorce? Empty nest? Magician? Crap! I can't read this! It's practically my life! My pathetic, going-nowhere life! Argggh!

I down half the wine, slam the book on the table, and the phone rings. The landline. The landline never rings! I hope everyone's okay.

"Hello?"

"Yes, hello. This is the Royal Bank of Canada. We would like to ask you if you're satisfied..."

"It's Saturday night! Are you fucking kidding me?"

"Uh, excuse me ma'am, sorry but we just have a few questions..."

"I'm very busy and very important, I'm sorry," I lie, punch the end button, slam the phone down on the table, and flop onto the sofa in frustration. Geesh! I miss the days when the phone rang, and it was an old friend, not a bank or an automated survey. I miss the days when the bulk of emails didn't disappear into your spam folder but were long notes from friends. I miss the 90s. I am officially old.

Maybe a little music. A little music never hurts. It can help me forget my pain.

I pick up the remote to my speaker system and turn on the first song on my playlist. Meghan Trainor's All About That Bass fills the room. I turn the volume as loud as it can go, toss off my shirt and unbutton my pants as I walk toward my room to change into something cozier.

The music is pounding as I pull on my flannel pink and yellow polka dot PJ's and furry pink slippers and tie my hair up in a high ponytail.

"Yeah, I'm pretty sure I ain't no size two!" I start to sing along with Meghan Trainor, and pick up the hairbrush to use as a microphone. Haven't done this in years. Could be a good release. Dance like nobody's watching... 'cause nobody is!

I moonwalk into the living room and wiggle my ass furiously, singing louder into the hairbrush: "You think you're fat, but every inch of you is perfect from the booty to the top...!"

I'm shaking my butt high up in the air, then kicking my feet like a young girl doing the can-can.

Only, I'm pretty sure I can't-can't.

I'm going to be sore tomorrow.

"Er... Mom? You okay? Mom!"

My youngest daughter, Alyssa, is standing in the front hallway, looking slightly stunned. She shouts louder to get my attention. I stop can-canning, toss the hairbrush on the couch, and cross my arms.

"Yeah... yeah, I'm fine! Just working out!"

"In your PJ's?" she says suspiciously. She walks up to the

stereo and turns the volume way down.

I wipe my brow, grab my wine glass, and collapse on the couch. She's got me.

"So, I was letting off a little steam. Don't you do that, or are Goths always chillaxed?" I never know whether to look into my 20-year-old's eyes anymore, or if she'll think I'm staring at her two eyelid piercings. Which, of course, I am – hoping they'll be gone, every single time. I want her to express herself, just not so... 'In Yo' Face!' When she first got the piercings, dyed her hair jet-black, and started wearing the black lipstick that's become a permanent fixture on her face, I thought it would be a two-week phase. Two weeks quickly melted into two years. I asked Cici what she thought I should do, and she said to punish her.

Punish an 18-year-old? She was about to leave home! I didn't have the right! Besides, she'd gone through enough punishment having Jimmy as a father. I'm certain some of his physical abuse led to this rebellion, er, self-expression. I decided to let her do what she wanted as long as it didn't get infected, or interfere with her getting a job. Of course, being brilliant Alyssa, she got the first job she applied for and has been able to pay for rent without any help from me or Gram. It surprises me that an accounting office took Lyssa on as their receptionist, but she tells me they're all "kinda grunge Goth" at this firm.

"Okay, sure. Maybe I need to hire them to do my taxes. They'll keep me in the black," I'd said to her.

"Hardy har-har." She'd rolled her eyes. "Like we haven't heard that one before."

How'd my baby grow up so fast? It feels like only yesterday

I was watching her walk to school for the first time with a group of older friends.

I remember the day well. Alyssa was eight. She'd been standing at the bus stop with me and Jenna, a cool September breeze giving us a chill at the back of our necks, reminding us summer was coming to an end. Jenna's good friend Shawna, also 11, started to walk past us. "I get to walk to school today!" she said.

The girls turned and gave me puppy dog eyes.

"We never walk to school," Jenna spoke for the both of them.

"Oh, how we wish we could!" Alyssa piped in, trying to sound poetic and grown-up.

The walk was a good 25 minutes. I didn't realize they wanted it this much, when they had a perfectly good bus to take. I thought about it for 30 seconds and did what any sane mother would do in that situation. I gave them each a kiss on the cheek, let them join Shawna, and called out, "I love you. I love you. I love you alllll!" to Jenna's great mortification as they walked away. Then, I called up the school secretary, Mrs. P., and freaked out for about four minutes, hoping to get her reassurance that they'd arrived there safely, and that she'd make sure they didn't walk home.

It was 8 a.m. Mrs. P. was about to do her daily vocal announcement over the intercom, "Ding-a-ling-a-ling! That's your bell!"

The school bell wasn't working because the school was still under construction for an expansion. Alyssa told me Mrs. P. did the 'Ding-a-Ling" announcement six times a day. I wondered if Mrs. P. got paid extra in those chaotic weeks of construction. Poor gal. At the very least, someone should give her a fancy sign for her desk: CEO of Sore Tummies, Snotty Noses, and Intercom Ding-a-Lings.

As much as I annoyed the school staff and embarrassed Jenna, that was the day, the hour, the minute that I started to let go: September fifth, when Alyssa was eight. I realized Jenna would be going to high school, soon, and I knew she needed to start doing these things on her own. That was logical. The harder part was convincing myself there were no Boogeymen hiding in the bushes waiting to attack a group of children on their way to school. And, if there were, what was I going to do about it? Chain them to their desks in their rooms until they were ready to move out? I knew I had to let my girls explore the world and make their own mistakes.

I had to let them go, just a little, just around the corner all the way to school, and I hoped with all my heart they'd come back to me.

They did come back to me, year after year, and even now that they live elsewhere, now that I've let them go, they return to me. Yet, they've grown so fast. People say blink and you'll miss it, but I can remember our one vacation in Maine in Technicolor. Out on the ocean with nowhere we had to be – that was the only time in my all-too-long abusive marriage when we felt completely free. Free from Jimmy's ridiculous rules, free from his shouting, his raging, his berating, the drugs and drinking, and best of all, free from the hitting.

The morning sun sparkled like diamonds through the thin fog as we made our way to the empty beach. A short walk along the sandy path near our car where we'd spent the night. The freshly raked sand was covered in minute stones that shimmered the full spectrum of colors in the sunlight. Small pools of water left from high tide rippled in the wind. Slowly, the sea receded in its lifelong argument with the moon; its white surf rushed rhythmically onto the sand like a battle cry, proof it held more strength and power than any other force on the planet. In the end, gravity won, and the sea rushed back out again.

Jenna and Alyssa ran to the raging surf, arms wide open, as if embracing their long lost friend. They tossed their sweatshirts, flip flops, and beach bags on the towel I'd laid out.

"Careful, girls! There could be rip tides! Stay shallow," I called. I wondered if I'd always be like a lighthouse, flashing warning signals to my girls, no matter what their age. Look both ways! Chew your food. Are you buckled up? Don't give out your address. Don't run beside the pool!

Mom: Always On Duty. It comes with the scars of childbirth, but I wouldn't mind if I could take a vacation from it, while on vacation. Unfortunately, it's pure instinct. You can't fight it, and it never goes away.

After ten minutes by the water, Alyssa left her sister's side, ran up to me, and lay down on my oversized beach towel. This wasn't like her. She was always so busy with creative projects, always socializing with the other children. She wasn't a worry-wart like me. She didn't have skeletons in her closet; she had Skittles, a secret diary, and a flashlight. Oh, to be nine.

She was quiet, brushing the sand off the top of her feet and flicking it from between her toes.

"What's up, pumpkin?" I asked. "Did you have a fight with Jenna?"

"No." She kept looking at her feet.

"Maybe you're hungry?" I asked. We'd packed enough muffins and drink boxes for our breakfasts, and with what little money I'd grabbed from my emergency Mason jar, we'd been able to afford fast-food dinners, but not much else. I felt a pang of guilt, until she answered.

"I'm fine. I just like sitting beside you, sometimes. That's all." She covered the top of her forehead like a visor, shading the sun from her eyes, and looked up to me, giving me a beautiful, lopsided, missing-two-teeth, grin.

It's not often I know when I'm doing a good job as a mother. It's easy to question that. In that small, fleeting moment, however, I knew I was doing okay. I wanted to tie that feeling up with a fancy ribbon to keep forever in a memory box. Instead, I took a mental photograph and let the moment pass as it should.

"I just like sitting beside you, sometimes, too," I answered, then took the small blue fan spray-bottle she'd picked up at the dollar store and turned it on right in front of her nose. She grabbed it and tried to spray my face in retaliation. Jenna came skipping up, piled onto us with her usual sense of abandon, and a full-on tickle fight ensued.

Alyssa flops down in the spot right beside me, rests her head on a pillow, and looks up at the wall. "Sorry I just swung by here unannounced, Mom."

"You know you're always welcome. Always. What's up?"

"I thought I was going to this party tonight, but it turns out I wasn't invited." She sighs, still staring up at the ceiling.

"What? I thought you were going with Brigitte and Annabelle. I thought you loved them."

"I do, okay? They just found this new crowd, and I don't really fit in with them. They didn't want to tell me I wasn't actually invited, so they texted me from the party."

"Wow. That's classy."

"Way of the world, Landline Lady. Get with the times."

"Hey, I text just like everyone else, but I need the landline in case Gram calls."

"Mom. Gram usually tweets you when she needs you. You'd know that if you used your phone more."

"Hey, can you be nice, here? Don't deflect attention to me. This is about you. Are you ok?" I try to take her hand, but she doesn't give me hers. She looks over at me, tears in her eyes.

"Yeah, whatever, I'll be fine." She keeps staring up at the ceiling, and for a brief moment I miss the little girl who would curl up to me and put her head on my shoulder whenever we sat together. She hugs a pillow and relaxes back further into the sofa.

"Whatever you want, honey," I say softly, sweeping the hair off her forehead. "Want some warm milk?"

"Uh, actually, Mom," she chuckles, "I'd love a glass of wine."

My baby's all grown up. I pour her a glass and hand it to her. When we raise and clink our glasses, we toast to "Change."

Chapter Four

Sunday, February 19, 2017

I wake up feeling like an elephant and a dump truck are playing bumper cars with my brain. Oh God, my head. Why do I always buy the cheap red wine?

Buzzzzz.

Great, a text. Please don't let it be something that takes me out of this bed. Let it be Jenna telling us she's bringing breakfast here.

I reach out in the darkness for my phone on the bedside table and feel a small crack on the case. Crap! Right. This is Cici's phone. We've switched them again. The only light in the room is a glowing text from my number. She's insisting I join her and Gram for Saturday brunch, an introduction, and a big announcement. I frown when I read the "introduction" part.

<C, uv already done enuf. Can't Wait Cam was bad. Top 40 Tom worse. Wrong Word Will last straw! NO more blind dates. WHERE do u meet these Mormons?>

<U meant morons, right? Not a blind date. It's my new editor! I have great news! Come eat & meet PLS? Brunch on me.>

Cici has freelanced as a food columnist for The Ottawa Citizen for almost five years, but recently, she's been telling me she wants "more." She says she doesn't feel fulfilled or important critiquing food. She's been joining Gram on Twitter and Facebook, and social networking for hours at a time every day. She's a total teenager. She even says she has an idea for a book about staying organized, for the over-40 crowd. I'm sure all of this has something to do with Empty Nest Syndrome, but when I brought it up, she disagreed. Vehemently.

"Empty nest? Are you nuts? Hallelujah, it's empty! Simon and I have the Best Sex *Ever* now! I can actually make noises!"

Too much information. *Way TMI*.

I agree to go to brunch, but make her promise she won't try to set me up with anyone ever again. She texts back 'Ok,' but it isn't that convincing. Can you text with one hand and cross your fingers behind your back at the same time? I wonder.

"Alyssa," I call to the other room, "I'm going out for brunch, want to join us?" Hearing no reply, I get out of bed and make my way to the pull-out couch. It's already been made, the sheet and blanket folded neatly on the arm rest, with a small yellow sticky note on top.

Thanks Mom. C ya soon. xox ~A

I smile at the note. It was a good Saturday night, after all. I hope she comes back to me again, soon. I must, however, make a mental note that she and Jenna still have keys.

The hairbrush singing has got to stop.

To my surprise, traffic is light. I got ready in record time. We're going to a fancy hotel for brunch with three courses and a buffet. Granny panties with 10 percent spandex, don't let me down.

When I finally get downtown, it's impossible to find parking on the street, so I hand the valet my car keys, enter the elaborately decorated lobby, and take the elevator straight up to the 21st floor. The view is stunning. I can see a section of the Ottawa River glistening in the sunshine and the top of the Parliament buildings.

Gram and Cici are already sitting at the corner table when I arrive. Cici's long, red hair shines like the river in the sun. She's dressed in a crisp ivory pantsuit that shows off her trim, long legs. I'm immediately jealous. Spaz that I am, I could never wear that. I'd just spill food on it in the first 40 seconds.

As usual, Gram, aka Kate Morgan or @BadAssGrandma, is getting a lot of attention from the waiters and passersby. She's graciously shaking their hands and signing autographs. Since her rise to fame with Badass Grandma on MTV, she usually wears dark glasses and a floppy black hat when out in public, but I know she often tires of that, and wants to be a normal person. "As normal as an eccentric old goat can be, anyways," she says. Today, she's dressed in her infamous attire: the made-to-measure velour jogging suit. This one is black and gold, and she's wearing matching running shoes. She's let her snow-white hair flow over her shoulders and down her back, and in this moment, as I see her smiling up at her adoring fans, she looks angelic. Almost.

The manager takes my red wool coat and leads me to the table. Along with the granny panties, I wore a stretchy red dress that makes me feel sexy and curvaceous with the hopes that its spandex sucks in any evidence of overeating. I know it's a lost cause. We modern women expect way too much from our fashion, our banks, our men, and most of all, ourselves. We're bound to be disappointed on a daily basis.

To make matters worse, women over 40 are made to believe that we're bound to disappoint most men if we don't use 18 Again cream to shrink our sagging vajayjays. Shame on us for growing older or giving birth! I think of my fantasy island, stocked with every kind of coffee imaginable. I can always go there in my mind. After brunch.

Be in the moment, Cat. Let go of these body insecurities. One brunch isn't going to turn me into the Pillsbury Dough Boy! I should relax and enjoy this spread, which is absolutely incredible. There's a buffet with mussels and salmon, another with salads, another with cold cuts, another with breakfast foods, and at the center of the room, a chef making omelets. To his left lies my greatest temptation: a chocolate fountain surrounded by colorful fruit. Are there rules for brunch? Can I skip the rest and start right at the chocolate fountain? Would anyone notice?

I manage to walk past the fountain and arrive at the table without drool down my chin. Cici stands to give me a quick hug, while Gram raises her coffee mug. She's enjoying some silence now that the manager has kindly asked that people leave her alone to eat in privacy.

"Hey, Cat, before I forget, here's your phone back, and I need mine." Cici hands me my teal blue phone and leaves her palm open in a request for hers, which happens to be the same color. This is why we've switched them three times this year, already.

"I promise I didn't read your texts. Well, maybe just three," she says, then sees me glaring at her. "Four. Okay, five! I read five. They weren't even juicy ones. Except Mark. He's that twenty-something guy you train at your gym? Was he flirting with you?"

I rummage through my purse and place Cici's phone in her hand before sitting down, with Gram in between us.

"Okay first off, that's just wrong that you read my texts. Second, I don't know if Mark is or isn't flirting with me, but he's a client, and he's half my age, so I can't even go there." I grab my cup, reach for the silver pot of coffee, and start pouring my first cup of the day. I shouldn't have waited until 11 a.m. for coffee. My brain isn't functioning right, yet.

"I'm forty-one. I consider myself a modern woman, but, you know how you once tweeted that you don't get this fascination with vampires?"

"I just write and post 'em, honey. Don't remember 'em. I'm ninety-four. Can't remember what color panties I have on."

"Well, anyway, like you don't get the fascination with vampires, I don't get this fascination with sexting."

"It doesn't do it for you?" Gram asks without hesitation, as though she's become a sexting expert. I don't wanna know.

"No, it doesn't do it for me, Gram. It confuses me! I don't know if a winky face is just a winky face, or an invitation to his place. Then he puts "!!!!!" when I asked what he thinks about adding another workout with me to his twice-a-week regime. It's so vague. Obviously, he's excited, but I definitely wouldn't call it foreplay."

"All those exclamation marks? Wow, Cat, he pretty much wants to jump your bones. Seriously." Cici's smirking.

"Even I know that," Gram interjects. "It's like he's advertising his boner."

"Gram!" I choke on my coffee, trying to resist the giant spurt. It's too late, the coffee has left my mouth and is headed for the boobs. Damn! I quickly dab them and my dress with my napkin, but the damage is done. There's a large, brown stain on my right breast.

Gram passes a crisp new twenty dollar bill to Cici. She doesn't even do it under the table. So cruel.

"I take it you made a bet? How long before I spilled food on my boobs? Right. Mature, family, very mature."

They're both chuckling. Cici's actually snorting a little. "Sorry, Cat, just having a little fun. Hey, we have to stop switching our phones like that. Maybe I'll bejewel mine so we can tell them apart." She lowers her voice. "But something great came out of the switch this time. I don't know how to explain it..."

"Can we eat first and gab later? I'm not gettin' any younger." Gram pushes herself up using the table and slowly walks away. Cici and I stop talking and watch her.

"She's slowed down a lot in the last few years," Cici says, lowering her voice even more, to a whisper. "You think she's okay living alone?"

I watch Gram pick up a plate, smile at the people in line in front who recognize her, and load her plate up with bacon. Just bacon.

"I think as long as her doctor says it's okay, and he has, and we keep taking her out at least once a week, she'll be fine. She's doing amazingly well for her age."

The waiter interrupts us with three menus for the plate part of our meal. We have a choice of veal, chicken or beef.

"I can't decide, so I'll just start with the buffet," I say.

Cici puts down her menu and looks at me. "Uh, sir, I think you missed giving my Gram over there the menu. Cat, you should order the chicken. I've had it before. It's remarkably great."

I give the waiter my menu and smile up at him. "My sister's a food columnist. She's got fancy ways to describe things. I just enjoy the eating part." I chuckle. "I'll have the chicken then, thanks." The waiter nods and leaves.

I take a sip of my coffee and look at Cici. "Remarkably great, huh? That's a new one. What exactly does that mean?"

"It's a phrase I use when you come across something that's like nothing you've ever experienced before. In a good way. Or, a great way." She gestures for me to get up. "For instance, this buffet we're about to try? It's pretty good. Sex with your twenty-something? That could be remarkably great. You could be missing out!" She links her arm in mine, but I push her away with my hip.

"Enough, Cici, I'm old enough to be his mother," I say, but I can't help laughing. Being with my sister always feels so freeing. I can just be myself. I wish I could spend more time with her.

"So," she continues under her breath as we walk toward the first buffet table, "Gram's extra quiet today. I'm not sure why. Maybe she's waiting to hear my news, but I thought you should know."

I peer ahead in line and see Gram has added eggs Benedict to her plate of bacon, and is shuffling off to her seat.

"Oh? Okay, I'll try to find out what's up. And what about this big news? It's a publishing deal, I assume. It's all you've talked about this last week. So, when do I get to meet this editor?" I take a plate from the pile and hand one to Cici. "I'm in total suspense. Spill!"

"Well funny you asked; he just walked in." She smiles as

I pile my plate high with pancakes and fresh blueberries and places her hand at my back so I have to turn around.

I think I'm in foodie heaven.

Or possibly, genie hell.

The man standing in front of me, the man Cici introduces as the editor she's been working with, has jet-black hair, a tanned complexion, piercing green eyes, an elaborate Celtic tattoo on his toned right bicep, and a charming, boyish smile. It's Gene. I can't believe it. Either he's Gene, or I've lost my mind.

I'm going to drop my pancakes all over the place.

"Cat." He keeps smiling, looking directly in my eyes, but doesn't give away our secret. He seems nervous. "I'm so pleased to meet you. Your sister's told me so much about you."

The room is starting to spin. I need to sit down. Gene senses this immediately and grabs my back with his left arm, trying to keep me from losing my balance. Of course, it's Gene. He's touching the small of my back, and my knees start to buckle even more.

"Please don't faint, Petal," he whispers in my left ear. "And, if Gram kicks me in the nuts again, I'm outta here."

There! He admitted it! It is him. What's going on? I'm feeling so woozy. I sit down at the nearest table, but it's not our table. The two children eating pancakes here are staring at me like I'm an alien. I put my head down on the empty white plate in front of me. At least it cools me.

"What did you do to her?" Gram's suddenly beside me, hands on hips, shaking a finger at Gene. "You disappear for years, break her heart, make her think she's gone crazy, and then you show up and make a scene in public like this?"

Gram doesn't realize she's the one making a scene in public. I suppose that's the life of a reality TV star.

Cici has taken the seat beside me, next to a large bald

headed gentleman. She looks pale. Pale and confused doesn't look pretty on a redhead. "You two know each other? He broke your heart? What the...?" She's trying to keep her voice low, without much success.

"Yeah, Cici, we do. Sorry I couldn't tell you that. Katherine, try to calm down. We should take this somewhere else. Somewhere more private." Gene's eyes are pleading with mine.

I can feel my blood pressuring rising and my heart rate quickening. Oh crap, my heart. I need to calm myself. This kind of shock can't be good for someone who's suffered a heart attack. I lift my head off the plate and look directly in his beautiful green eyes.

"You want me to calm down? *Calm down?* You disappear for almost four years, and you want to take this somewhere else? You're seriously going to make me wait even longer for an explanation, Gene?"

Gene glances over at the children and bald man, who have stopped eating and are soaking us in like the latest Netflix craze. "Petal," he whispers, "I tried to come back to you. I did everything I could. Let me explain."

"Sure. Do you have four years? Because you've got that much explaining to do!" I yell. I can't help it. We've lost so much time, and here he is, calling me Petal, expecting me to pick up where we left off.

I should calm down; he's right. I should be more fair. He did make me wish myself back to health when I was hit by the car. He gave up his one chance for freedom when he did that. Maybe he really has been trapped all this time. I just don't get why he's been posing as Cici's editor.

People are starting to gather around our table. Gram slams her hands down on the table, stands up, and speaks to the crowd. "What's happening here is really none of your business, people. But since I once made it my business to share with you, I'll forgive you for being interested. Here's the thing: my show hasn't been picked up for another season. It's done. Over. Kaput. So you all need to move along, now. Give an old lady some space."

"Come on, Cici," Gram continues, "Let's leave these two love birds alone. I'll explain everything to you over at the dessert table.

Cici looks at Gram like she has died and come back to life. She opens her mouth, but nothing comes out. Finally, she finds her words. "Your show's been canceled? Oh, Gram. And, you... you know everything? What's there to know? What'd I miss?"

"Oh about thirty years. Yeah. About that. A whole lifetime actually. It will boggle your mind. It's a good story, though. Strangely, incredibly good. Come on, sweetheart, you're gonna need ice cream."

When they're both gone, Gene takes Cici's seat. The bald man has continued eating his meal, but the kids are still watching us like we're the hired entertainment.

"I don't want to do this, here," Gene says. "Please, can we go to your place?"

"It sounds like you've been at Cici's place a while," I say. "You sure you won't need your silk PJs and toothbrush?"

"Oh, for God's sake, Katherine, it's not like that! Can't you be a grown-up, here, and let me explain?" Gene runs his fingers through his hair in frustration.

Cici storms toward us. I swear she's going to dump her plate of chocolate-covered strawberries all over Gene's head. Instead, she slams the plate down on the table and puts her hands on her hips. "You should have told me you'd been her genie, too. You should have explained about you two. I'd never have taken you on if I'd known the whole story."

Huh. One trip to the chocolate fountain, and Cici knows

I've fallen in love with a genie. I doubt it'll be this easy when I have to explain it to the girls.

"I'm not allowed to divulge anything about previous clients, Cici. I've broken the rules before, but this time… this time, I'm so close to freedom, I had to stick to the contract."

"Oh, is that why you're finally back, Gene?" I stand beside Cici, crossing my arms. "You need help being set free? So you're back to use us, and then disappear again, is that it?"

Gram's returned, and she doesn't look pleased. In fact, she's taking something out of her purse. It's a Ziploc bag.

"Forty-nine-ninety-five for all you can eat, my ass. I waited for my main plate for a half hour. The service here sucks. Next life, I'm gonna ask to be born with a built-in bullshit detector."

She turns to look directly at me and Cici. "Children. We need to leave. This is getting overheated. I'm not interested in reading about what we ate and argued about in Star Magazine, right beside George and Amal's Most Brilliant & Beautiful Baby photos. Cici, drive me home. Gene, you're under Cici's command, let's go."

Gram stuffs her Ziploc bag with bacon and chocolate-covered strawberries, seals it, and puts it in her purse. "Cat, you can be angry all you want, but sooner or later you need to decide if you want this – him – in your life again. You have a choice, cupcake. Make the right one."

She turns and walks off with Cici falling behind her miming 'call me!'. She doesn't dare mess with the matriarch of this family. Gene looks right through me. He has tears in his eyes. I've never seen him look so frustrated, powerless, and sad. He follows Cici out the door and doesn't look back.

I'm left at the table with Bald Guy and two beaming children. The little boy is coloring a picture of a genie with purple smoke whirling around what looks like a plate of scrambled eggs. I stuff a chocolate covered pineapple piece in my mouth and try to digest what transpired.

Well, my life certainly isn't boring, anymore.

Chapter Five

Kaboom! There's the thunder.

I throw my keys on the small table in the front hallway and hang up my barely damp coat, then turn to look out the living room window at the rain falling hard and fast against the pane. I'm glad I got home before the downpour started.

Okay. I need tea.

I fill the kettle and flick the switch, grab my favorite red mug from the cupboard, and toss in an Orange Pekoe teabag. Gene would berate me about making tea like this. He'd say,

"You have to give it a better chance, a chance to enjoy its full flavor. You have to make a full pot with tea leaves, and let them steep. You can't rush something that can be so much better if you wait."

Wait? For a better chance? I didn't give him much of anything, just now. Why did I do that? I turn to look at myself in the mirror. My eyes are still puffy from crying on the drive home. Why didn't I even let him speak? I got so angry, seeing him in my world, when he's been absent for so long. It came as such a shock. I don't need this. Not right now.

So many years being ridiculed by people because of my weight. So many years being mocked and slapped around by Jimmy. I got so used to being treated like shit, expecting all men to treat me that way, because most of them did. But now, now I have to stop thinking like that. I have to give Gene the benefit of the doubt. He saved me. He saved my life. He deserves a better chance.

The kettle's boiling. I pour the water into the mug and take it into the living room. The rain is still coming down hard; there's distant rumbling and little shards of lightning flecking the dark blue sky. As I sit down on the sofa, the doorbell rings. I know exactly who that is. We have a sixth sense about each other. Should I answer it?

I practically rush to open it. We need to fix this!

Gene is standing at the door, completely drenched. His hair is matted against his head and one strand has fallen straight across his left eye. He blinks as I sweep it back for him and attempt a smile.

"Get in here. You're soaked!"

He kicks off his shoes inside the doorway, and without saying a word, follows me through to the kitchen.

"Yeah, well, that's what happens when you walk eight

blocks in the pouring rain."

"You walked? Why didn't you come on over here in a whirl of purple smoke?"

"Katherine, you know I don't get to use my own will. If I did, I'd have willed myself over here ages ago." I don't know what to say, and he doesn't seem to like the silence, so he blurts, "Cici told me to get over here. So I walked. Kinda ran a bit, actually."

"You walked through this rainstorm for me?"

"For you. For us. I needed to think. Cici didn't give me an umbrella. She's mad at me, too."

"I'm not really mad, Gene. I'm confused. We need to talk."

He looks at me a moment, his sad eyes roaming, like he's studying my every feature, preparing to paint it. "No." He takes off his wet coat and tosses it over the back of a kitchen chair. I let it drip on the floor. "No," he says again, "I think that's a very bad idea. We should talk later." He pushes me gently against the counter, looks deep into my eyes, and covers my mouth with his.

I'm immediately lost. Lost in his scent, that musky, earthy smell, lost in the rough touch of his unshaven chin against mine, lost in memories of how well our bodies fit together. I relax into it all.

"Wait!" I pull away from his kiss. Damn it, sensible side. Damn you! "Why didn't you come back to me? Why return to Cici?"

Gene steps back and takes a deep breath. He has an intriguing look on his face: he's lustfully irritated. "I did try to come back to you. Of course I tried! I've been trapped in your fucking phone. Only, it turns out your phone was actually over at Cici's. You two switch phones often?"

Oops. "Uh, yeah. Yeah, we do. That was kind of brilliant, to come to me on my phone. So. You wanted me to be your master again?" That phrase turns me on almost as much as his mouth did earlier.

"You'd think so. I have to be someone's genie one more time before I'm a free man. So, I asked to be returned to you – to your phone and your app. There are no rules against returning to a master. No genie's done it before, from what I can tell, but it's not against the rules, either. I thought I had it all figured out, but you never swept the right app, your battery kept dying, and then you'd leave your phone at Cici's. She ended up being the one to sweep the app." He sighs and rubs his forehead. "So, she is my most recent, and hopefully last, master."

"Genie of the App, huh? What app?"

He groans and looks down at his feet, slightly embarrassed. "Angry Birds, okay? I thought you played that!"

"Oh, yeah. Well, I did for a while, but then it got boring." A loud thunderbolt makes me jump, and I move closer to Gene. His scent and warmth draw me in again. I kiss him. His wet hair cools my face, which I know is flushing red.

I hug him tight. "I'm sorry I didn't let you explain," I whisper. "I've missed you, so much. There are no words. It's like I can start breathing again." His presence rushes through my body like a dose of morphine... calming. My calm during the storm.

"I missed you more, Cheesy girl," he says. "Let me add to our big block of cheese and say, how 'bout we do some heavy breathing, baby?" He chuckles at his own joke.

I love how he lets me be a cornball. I don't even laugh. I'm too turned on. Instead, I look up at him, deep into his green eyes, and wrap my arms tight around his waist. I am most myself when I'm with you. I don't have the courage to say this out loud, Gene, but yes, yes, do what you will with me. I'm yours. All yours...

Gene starts kissing my chin, my throat, and all the way

around to the nape of my neck, where his hand finds the zipper to my dress. It's off and on the floor in seconds. Oh My God. I'm in a Bridget Jones movie. This is so embarrassing. The granny panties!

Gene doesn't care. He stands back and stares at my big, black ensemble a few moments, his eyes widening with delight.

"Beautiful," he says. "Never better."

He grabs my ass with both his hands and hoists me up onto the counter.

Mmmm. I love feeling his hands on my skin after all this time. I wrap my legs around his torso and gently rub his shoulders. Now his mouth, nose, and chin are nuzzled into my breasts. He slowly licks the soft skin with his tongue and caresses them with one hand as he snaps off my bra with the other. Gently biting his lower lip, I pull at his shirt, trying to tug it off without unbuttoning it. A button pops off the bottom as I rip it over his head. "Oops." I giggle and start unzipping his pants. He pulls down his boxers. In seconds, he's standing in front of me, completely naked.

I can't stop staring.

He's delicious.

Gene takes my panties with the palm of his hands and rolls them off my hips and down my legs... Ever. Oh. So. My. Slowly.

God! I groan with impatience. He loves to make me wait for it, and the anticipation is so sweet. I throw my head back, grip onto the counter, lift my hips, and hold my breath until after what seems like a month. It escapes as a loud groan.

The counter is fine to begin with, then somewhat restrictive, and I soon find myself being carried into the bedroom.

The squeaking is a surprise. I've never made love on this bed before. I bought it when I got the condo. It's cheap, but comfortable. Very comfortable, right now. We're chuckling every time the headboard squeaks. It makes a loud sound, but it isn't interfering with our pleasure. It's heightening our excitement, if anything. His eyes sparkle, and I hold them steady in mine, as I rise and fall onto his body.

Squeak! Squeak! Moan.

I look down at Gene. My hair has fallen in front of my face, my tummy's touching his, I'm hot, perspiring, and I know my mascara's run, but none of that matters because of the way he's looking at me. I'm a hot mess, and it feels fantastic.

Gene locks his eyes with mine before he puts his hands at my waist and rolls me over. We groan with pleasure as we rock together, slowly at first, then faster, harder, wilder. I can hardly contain this searing ecstasy. I reach for the side of the headboard with one hand, and with the other, I smack the mattress. The heat builds and builds until I call his name and blissful relief floods in, washing over me like cool rain on an August evening.

I fall forward onto the mattress, roll over, and rest my head on Gene's heaving chest. Leaning over, he kisses my lips, nose, and eyebrows before falling back against his pillow. We're staring up at the ceiling in silence except for our throbbing hearts. As our breathing falls into beautiful unison, we're about to fall into a blissful sleep...

Squeak... *Thunk!*

"Oh!" I sit up fast, pulling the sheet against my breasts. Ouch! That was a jolt to my back. "Is someone here? What just happened?"

Something's wrong. Unbalanced. The bottom half of the bed has sunk down to the floor! Gene has a giant grin on his face. He begins to shake, choking back his laughter.

"Guess what? Honey? We broke the bed."

Chapter Six

"Push! Push! You can do it! Push harder!"

Gene's commands take me back to the day Jenna was born, and it makes me snort-laugh, which doesn't help matters.

I'm sitting on the floor, back against the sunken bed, my legs wide apart, bare feet pushing against the wall. There's one part, however, that's rather different from giving birth. There's been no epidural, and this pushing is grueling work.

Someone give me the freakin' drugs!

Gene is laughing, too, and alternately muttering, "Quit it!

I have to concentrate on this!" He's using me to leverage the bed so he can get under it to try to straighten the broken leg. An excellent plan, in theory. Only, it's not working, and I'm about to give birth to a 10 lb baby.

"Let's take a breather, Petal," he says, getting up off the floor and pulling me up with one hand. "This isn't exactly what I envisioned we'd be doing after our reunion in the sheets."

"Oh no? I put all my men to work afterward. They need to know who's boss." I smirk and motion him to follow me to the kitchen. He looks around, grabs a pink fleece robe hanging at the back of my bedroom door, and wraps it around his chest.

"It suits you," I say. I'm already cozy in my favorite white waffle robe.

"It's just until the living room, don't get too excited." Still, he turns in a full circle and wiggles his hips like a woman would, modeling the pink fleece in jest.

"We can cuddle up by the fire in there." He reaches out for my hand, and I place my palm against his. I'd forgotten how much I missed that.

The rain is still coming down in buckets, but I like it. Sunday afternoon rain always makes me feel more alive, if I can fight off the urge to stay in bed all day. It's brightening up a little outside. There's half a rainbow behind the neighboring building. We stand side by side in complete silence and watch it for a while. After a few minutes, I head into the kitchen and start the kettle to make us hot chocolate. Gene stays silent, except for a few contented sighs.

I place our steaming mugs on the coffee table and take one side of the couch. He takes the other, stretching out his legs so they brush against me. His toes start dancing with mine, and I start to giggle.

"Careful, sailor, we don't have a bed, so don't get too

frisky."

"Bed? Who needs a bed?" He raises his left eyebrow. Just his left eyebrow. I love when he does that.

Gene takes a sip of his hot chocolate, then wipes the whipped cream off his top lip. "Earlier, you mentioned all your men..." His voice trails off with self-awareness and a touch of vulnerability, but his eyes don't leave mine.

I knew he hadn't liked hearing that. "Okay, so this is when I list the many partners I've had since we had to part ways?" I frown, as though I've lost count. He's waiting for a number.

"Oh let's see, that would be... zero."

Gene looks relieved. He chuckles. "God! I never thought this'd be so important to me! I mean we're adults, and it's the twenty-first century. I'd understand if you had," he says. "I just thought we... you know. I love you."

"Oh, Gene, I think deep down, I always knew that." I start tearing up. "It's good to hear it again. I've got to ask you the same question, though. It's only fair. Plus, I care. Did you go see her?"

I don't need to be specific. We both know I'm talking about his wife. She died shortly after giving birth to their son, but when Gene and I discovered his skills included time-travel, albeit a rocky, messed-up version of time-travel, I knew he'd try to get back to her when she was still alive. It's what I would do with my parents, if I could. It would be my one chance to say everything that didn't get said.

Gene places his hot mug on the table and reaches out for my free hands. "Yes, Katherine, I did go, but I only had what would feel like twenty-four hours to you. Twenty-four hours and three wishes as a reward for saving you, Logan, and Ben. It took a little over a full day in my world, but in your time, my absence probably felt like four years. Then, I was sent back to stasis, but got to choose where, and I chose your phone."

"Oh." I choke back tears. "That must have been bittersweet, Gene." I can't imagine being given just one day with Gene amid our years of separation, then losing him again. I found it beautifully painful receiving the red rose bouquet, wrapped in a pale yellow gossamer ribbon, with the small typed tag, "K & E – May 4, 2017," as a hint about our future wedding day in Mornas. It must have been tragic to see his wife for just a wrinkle in time.

"It gave me what I wanted. I needed closure and clarity. I got both. And then a little too much time in the dark." He still looks melancholy.

"Oh!" I'm hit with a sudden realization.

"You've hardly had time to miss me!" Here I was, a pathetic blob of a woman, dancing alone to Top 40 songs on a Saturday night, and Gene had hardly blinked!

"No, no. Don't think that way. Time doesn't affect me like it affects you. If I miss you, I miss you. It doesn't matter for how long."

He looks right into me.

"And, for the record, I missed you, Katherine."

"Do... do you want to hear about it?" He pulls me with his hands over to him, and I snuggle into him, my right cheek comfy inside the curve of his neck. He pulls the throw high up to my chin and wraps his arms tight around me.

"Yes," I whisper. "Don't leave anything out."

Chapter Seven

Gene

When you left me on that road in 1993, I was immediately thrown into stasis and assumed I'd be given a new master. Instead, the voices spoke to me. They told me I had saved three lives and was being granted three wishes of my own. At first, I thought I'd use one of those wishes to see you again, but then I came up with my plan to return to you as your genie. First, though, I needed to get some closure on an issue that had been weighing heavy on my heart.

I closed my eyes and wished for a chance to talk with my wife, Amara. "Take me to a time before our son was born, before I lost her," I wished out loud.

At first, nothing happened. It was cold, dark, and silent. I thought the voices had decided not to grant me my wish.

There was a rumbling noise and a flash of light, and I felt the world spin as my mind lifted through stasis and planted itself elsewhere. When I opened my eyes, I found myself in a dark, windowless, one-room home, furnished only with one bed and a wooden table. There was a wine decanter, empty glasses, half a loaf of fresh bread, and some fruit on the table. It looked like we'd just had a meal. I recognized it was the home where our son was born, but I didn't know what year it was, or if Amara was home. It was rather empty.

The door opened and my bride walked in. Dressed in a simple chiton, her hair shone with the pale orange morning light filtering through the door behind her. She wore field daisies as a wreath on top of her head and a smile that lit up the darkened room. She called to me like we'd never been parted. Of course, from her perspective, we hadn't.

"Eugenius, let's walk into town for lunch, today. I have some news; it would fare well to tell you on our way." For as long as we'd known each other, Amara and I had taken walks along the country road from our small village all the way into Athens. At first, they were to escape our elders and later, when we were married, to sort out our problems. This time, I didn't wonder what the concern was; I knew. I remembered this day. It was that Friday in 325 BC. How could I forget?

I was being given a second chance to right a lifetime regret.

I walked up to Amara and kissed her gently on the forehead. "The farm is in good shape. I'm all yours, today," I said, knowing full well there were a dozen chores I should tend to. The last time I lived this day, I'd told Amara I was too busy, and she could tell me her news while we were working in the field.

It was a warm summer day, so we changed into our lightest of chitons and sandals, and set out along the country road into town. I held her hand and listened attentively – like it was the last time I would hear her voice, because, it was.

When we were about half-way to Athens, Amara asked to rest by the river. We sat down on a grassy hill, and she splashed some water on her legs and feet.

"Eugenius." She looked into my eyes, and though I knew what was coming, I felt the anticipation of a life-changing moment in my quickened heartbeat. "I am with child." She smiled proudly. "I feel it's a son. Do you think one can know these things?"

"Oh Amara, you are his mother, you know." I kissed her, holding her tightly as I wept. She seemed surprised at my reaction, and in turn, she wept, too.

Usually, I withheld emotion around Amara. I needed to feel like the strong one, but I wanted her to know this mattered. Having a son – our son – mattered. I hadn't told her that last time. I had only said we'd have to work harder on the farm to afford one more mouth to feed. I'd been such an—

Chapter Eight

Cat

"Idiot?" I have to interrupt Gene. I have to. I've been listening intently to his story, but I can't believe he treated his pregnant wife like that.

"Yes, I was an idiot back then, okay?"

"Back then?" I smile. I don't want my genie to be getting a skyscraper-sized ego because he's all-powerful and the sex is so great.

"Nice one. Clever you." He gives me a gentle squeeze at my hip. "Yes, I can be stubborn and evasive, and I screw the magic up, okay? But at least now I know to take nothing – no one – for granted. At the time, I didn't know how lucky I was. I was always worried about money. I told you, that's why I had to go back and get some closure! Right my wrongs."

"Okay, but did it work?"

"Yes. It was a blissful day. We strolled the colonnade in the city and met up with a friend. I explained Amara was pregnant, and he offered to lend us his horse and wagon. At first, Amara resisted, telling me she was perfectly capable of walking home just as well as she had into town, but I insisted. Once home, I prepared a special dinner of bread dipped in wine, fruit, vegetables, and fish. We spent the night talking until she fell asleep in my arms."

"Oh. Women drank wine when they were pregnant in those years? Also, you cooked for her? Nice!" I smack his arm on his bicep, which is so firm, I know it can't hurt.

"The cooking? That's what you're most jealous of?" Gene laughs. "You! I told you I'd do the same for you, one day."

"One day, huh?" I get up off the sofa. "Brunch was a bust. We've hardly eaten all day, and I'm famished. What about now? Can you whip something up?"

"I'm famished, too." He gets up, stretching. "What do I have to work with?"

"Er, that might be a bit of a problem," I muse out loud. "Let me join you in the kitchen and see if I can't find some veggies and meat that aren't getting up and walking away."

Gene looks amused, but says nothing. As I begin rummaging through the fridge, he taps me on the arm to get me to turn around.

"You've got a fresh loaf of bread here and a lonely-looking

fondue pot up there that looks like it's never been used. You got cheese?"

"Yes!" I get up. "All that talk about bread dipped in wine? I could totally go for fondue."

"Let's do it, then. But I'm putting you to work. Here, chop this up." He hands me the loaf of bread and starts opening the fondue pot box.

"So, you said you were given three wishes. After you left Amara..."

"Ah yes, the story. Keep chopping, and I'll tell you the rest."

Gene

I left Amara the next morning while she was sleeping. She looked like an angel. Choking back tears, I closed the door behind me, knowing I couldn't wake her and say goodbye. I wanted to tell her I loved her one more time. I wanted to tell her how beautiful, and smart, and brave our son, Theodosius, would be, but of course, she'd think I'd lost my mind.

I couldn't tell her she would die shortly after giving birth to him, and there was no way to save her from that infection. I couldn't use my wishes to mess with time. We'd tried that before, and you and I got lucky. I didn't want to push my luck.

Once outside, I strolled the winding country road toward town, wondering how to make my next wish a reality. With us, you take my hands and make the wish, but it was different for me. I had to say it out loud. I sat under an oak tree and tried to find the right words so I wouldn't mess up my wish. After a few minutes, I had them.

"I wish to return to Mornas on May fourth, two thousand and seventeen."

I was sure that would do it. You'd be there; I'd be there; we'd be married in the castle. But, I screwed up, again. Cat... I missed the damn wedding!

Cat

"*Wait.*" I push Gene's hand away from the fondue pot and glare at him. "You're telling me you were there? You were *there*, and we're still *here?* What the hell happened?"

Gene dips his bread in the cheese, places it on a side plate on the coffee table, and looks at me.

"I don't know. I should have specified a time, I guess. The wedding had already happened when I got there. There were red rose petals on the ground, and I found that bouquet with the yellow ribbon that a bridesmaid must have tossed aside. I had no idea how to get to you, and besides, I wasn't allowed. I was being called to return to stasis, so I decided to send you a message. I wished to leave that bouquet for you to find on the passenger seat of your car.

"The next thing I knew, I was completely in the dark. My momentary freedom was over; it was time to be someone's genie again. The voices told me I could choose where I was found, but I wasn't given long to decide. After all I went through with the Kardashians years ago, I'd completely had it with that Wii machine. I figured your cell phone was the perfect place for you to find me. Only, it wasn't." He gives me a look, his eyebrows are furrowed.

"Yeah," I say sheepishly, "I wish I'd switched my phone back with Cici sooner. She's had my phone for a few days, so I got so used to using hers, I kept forgetting to switch back."

"It's alright. We're together, now. That's what matters. Maybe that timeline in May will never pan out, now. Maybe it's not our destiny. Maybe things have changed, and we aren't meant to—"

"Shhhh!" I kiss him hard on the mouth to shut him up. He doesn't resist. After a minute, I continue my thoughts. "Don't say it! I've waited so long, dreamt about that day for so long. I thought I might never see you again, Gene. Don't say we aren't meant to be together." I toss the pillow that's been on my lap onto the sofa, stand up, and start to walk to the bedroom. I need to be alone.

"Petal, wait, I didn't mean we aren't meant to be together, I meant..."

I turn to look at him. "Don't you want to go? Don't you want to be in Mornas on that day this year, to see what happens for us?" Tears are falling down my face. Doesn't this matter to him?

"But 'us,' that's happening right now." Gene gets up, walks to me, and grabs my waist. "We need to live in the moment from here on out."

"So you can take or leave the wedding bouquets and old castles in France so long as you get Naked Cat?"

"Of course not! If you want the wedding in France, we'll try to make that happen for you." He leans in for a kiss, but I pull away.

"For me? For me?" I'm fuming. "This isn't one of my three wishes, Gene, those are long gone. This is supposed to be something we both want."

Gene gently wipes some tears off my cheek with his thumb and tries to pull me in close, though I'm resisting. I'm not really angry with him; I'm confused about our future. I wish I had all the answers, but do any of us? No. No one ever does. As life would have it, everything is usually made clear in hindsight, after we've already royally screwed up.

I'm about to relent and melt into his delicious kisses again when we're interrupted by a door slamming, and footsteps coming our way. My feisty red-headed sis is standing before us, shaking her red umbrella out all over my wood floor.

"Does *nobody* in this family knock, anymore?" I shout at my sister in frustration.

"Uh, well, I had the key, so..." Cici's out of breath, and her cheeks are flushed red. She looks more excited than embarrassed, though. "I'm so sorry to interrupt you two!"

I pull out of Gene's embrace and take Cici's damp umbrella from her, placing it upright in the far corner of the hallway. She brushes off her wet, red trench coat. More droplets land on my floor. Grrr. Since when did I care so much about keeping my place neat? Oh right, since I started paying the bills all by myself.

"Nope, not interrupting anything. In fact, Gene was just leaving." I glare at him.

"Petal," Gene's pleading at me with his eyes. "We can do the wedding. I just felt maybe we were rushing things a little."

"Not interrupting? You're eating fondue in bath robes, talking about your wedding." Cici's biting her lip, holding back her laughter. "And Gene's in a pink, fleece one." Here come the giggles. "I should really come back later."

I ignore Cici and look at Gene. "Rushing things? Gene, I've been waiting nearly four years for you!"

"But Katherine, we've hardly even dated, yet." He comes closer and wraps his arms around me. "Is it so wrong that I want to take you out to dinner? Travel a little? I want to live my life with you as an ordinary man. Not as a genie."

I hate it when he makes sense. I hate that. But I wanted my fancy wedding in France! Why does he have to talk sense into me? Why?

"That does sound like something you'd tell the girls, Cat." Cici is sitting on the sofa, helping herself to leftover fondue. Sisters. "You wouldn't want them to rush into marriage, either."

"Cici?" I sit down beside her, shove her over a little, and stuff a piece of bread in my mouth. Conflict always makes me hungry. "Mffph. Why are you even here? Have you come to collect your Genie of the... App?" I'm frustrated, but I still have a hard time saying that and not cracking up.

Cici snickers. "No, silly, he was yours first, so I thought we'd share him."

"Ew. That's really kinky." I look over at Gene, who's still standing. He's turned bright red.

"I'm open minded but that's just—" Before he can finish his sentence, Cici finishes for him.

"Ew! Guys, no. Simon and I, we're good, thanks. I just meant we should wish my last two wishes together, Cat. I wished for my book about organizing social networking to be published, and thanks to Gene, it was. It's out there on the shelves as we speak. I didn't get to tell you about it at brunch because Gene took you by surprise." Cici pulls a hardcover book from her oversized purse. The title *On Top of It!* is printed in bold, white block letters across a photo of a cell phone and laptop sitting side by side.

"Oh, Cici, congrats!" I lean in and give her a hug. "I love how it's about organization, but the title could be about sex."

"We thought it was rather clever. Gene helped." She smiles.

"I know you wanted to do something more than your food column, and I was always proud of you for that. Now, I'm happy you're happy."

Gene joins us on the far side of the sofa. "I'm pleased I could help two sisters in this family," he says.

"The thing is... Oh, I don't know. Oh, Fuckity! I'm not. I'm not happy!" Suddenly, Cici bursts into tears. Her face looks like a squashed tomato. If this is what perimenopause does, I want no part of it. But of course, genetics being what they are, I'm doomed.

"I thought being published would solve all my anxiety." Cici grabs a Kleenex from the box on the side table and loudly blows her nose. "But I'm still anxious. All. The. Time! I don't know why it is, Cat." She begins biting her right pinky nail, inhales and starts to express another thought as her cell phone rings.

"Just a sec." She digs into her purse and takes out her cell. "Hello? Steph. Hi honey. Listen, we're all going to a casino tonight – me, Gram, Cat and her girls – can you join us? Do you know if your sister's free?"

"*What?*" I yell at Cici, despite that she's still talking to her eldest daughter.

Cici puts her hand over her phone for a minute. "Oh, yea, I forgot to tell you what my second wish is. I want to win two million at Wynn Casino in Vegas! Wouldn't that be a hoot? Way more fun than Gene just handing the money over to me! Eeeeek! I'm so psyched!" She uncovers the phone and continues talking to Stephanie.

Honestly, there are days I wonder who the older sister is. I know I'm already tired and it's only 8 p.m., so I am sure my grandmother is fast asleep. Cici wants to wake Gram and wish us all over to Vegas to win money? What happened about us making the next wish together? I reach out for Gene's hand, pull him off the sofa, and practically drag him back to my bedroom.

"I want you too, babe, but you don't have to be so forceful." He leans in to kiss me. "Unless you want it that way."

"Stop it Gene. We have to discuss something."

"I know. The wedding. Listen..."

"No! We don't have time for that, now. We have to stop her. She's making the same mistake I did with my first wish! I was vain. She's being materialistic. This isn't going to get us anywhere!"

"It could get us to Vegas, and I've never been." He puts his hands on my behind and rubs it. "We could have some fun together," he says, and tries to kiss my neck.

"Gene!" I wiggle out of his embrace. "Really! I learned to use the wishes for more important matters. Can't we share that lesson with Cici?"

"Nope." He pulls me back in and kisses me lightly on the lips. "She has to make her own mistakes, just like everyone else."

"But we'll be along for the ride..."

"Looks like it. Better strap yourself in," he says with a grin, just as Cici opens the door that I left slightly ajar.

"Oh!" Cici accidentally drops her phone and puts one hand over her mouth, but it doesn't stop the laughter from bellowing out of her mouth and echoing across the room.

"Now I know what made you two work up such a hunger! You broke the bed!"

Chapter Nine

"Ooh, how romantic. This is like something out of a movie!"

Cici is dressed in a sky blue sequined strapless gown. She looks like an A list actress, complete with an elaborate up-do and bright red lipstick. She's lowered the back window to our black stretch limo and is waving to people on the street as we drive through the darkened streets to our destination. The people aren't waving back.

"Yeah, well real life isn't a movie. I've been living a strange existence for years. I'd like some reality for a change," Gene grumbles.

He does look delicious, I'll give Cici credit for that part. He's in a classic tux with a black bow tie and gold cuff links. His black hair is slicked back and parted in a severe side part that accentuates his square jaw line. He looks like a leading man. My leading man. I'm so lucky. I give his hand a squeeze, and he squeezes mine back.

I didn't think I was as glamorous as Cici, but the way Gene is looking at me with those piercing green eyes makes me feel like a movie star. The whisperings of Ledussa, my Godess of Self-Loathing, are barely audible over the thumping of my happy heart, and I haven't thought once about my muffin top!

Okay, I just thought about it, but one moment of weakness since reuniting with Gene is not too shabby. I found self-love again when I opened my own gym and started helping others love themselves and their bodies. I don't need Gene or any man to tell me I look good. I've stopped comparing myself to Photoshopped models in magazines. I finally believe in myself... most days...after a jolt of java.

The way Gene looks at me gives me an extra glow. He makes me feel how I look after a blissful day on the beach. Plus, tonight, thanks to my best friend Mr. Ten Percent Spandex, I feel hugged in all the right places. This short, black cocktail dress and matching purse are lovely, but the antique silver pendant and matching dangly earrings are stunning. When Gene grants a wish that involves glamour, he doesn't hold back. I'd put money on a bet that he once lived in the Golden Age of Hollywood.

After we left the bedroom, Cici grabbed Gene's hands and wished our family could "all enjoy a glamorous evening at the Wynn Casino, where we'd come home with two million dollars." The whirl of purple smoke that brought the three of us and Gram into the limousine was a phenomenal sight. I will never get used to that.

"What the fuck am I doing here?" Gram has been asking

that repeatedly for the last two minutes, but Cici simply answers her with, "It's my wish. You're in it. Deal with it, Gram." I love their warm relationship.

"You got me out of bed, made me miss the end of Dancing With the Stars, and what the hell is this sparkly shit on my dress? It'd better be one hell of a wish, girly." Gram tries to brush off the sparkles on her golden gown. They aren't budging. At least Gene was wise enough to omit the heels and give her golden running shoes. I wish I had a pair of those. I'm afraid these strappy black stilettos are going to kill my back tonight.

"Oh, we should call everyone we know and have them join us!" Cici is scrolling through her contacts on her phone. "The girls, of course! Wait, does that still work for the wish?" She turns to Gene.

"Sure, you said "my family," so I could still bring any relatives into the wish, but we have to do it soon."

She's out of control. I know why she was never able to write a book on organization herself: that phone is actually glued to the palm of her hand, making her incapable of writing a word. "My kids are studying," she adds, "but I'm calling Jenna and Alyssa to see if they're free."

"Oh sure, ruin Cats' kids' studies, but not yours. That's smart," Gram interjects. I notice she's been sticking her tongue out the window at passersby. Nice.

"Jenna isn't answering, but I have Alyssa here. Hey Alyssa. Want to join us at a casino?"

I grab Cici's phone and give her a look. "Lyssa, it's Mom. Oh? Never mind, you have fun; I'm glad you're included this time."

I hand Cici back her phone. "How on earth were you going to explain to her that we were going to a casino tonight, but not one *in this city?*"

Cici smiles. "It's time Cat. You should call her back. She needs to know about Gene! Get all your skeletons out of the closet, but hide your negligee, because that will disgust her. Our kids don't think we have sex anymore. Hang on..."

I'm pleased to learn Lyssa is going to a little gathering tonight. Perhaps those new friends are finally including her. Still, I feel a little on edge. I'm not sure why. I look up at Gene. "I'd like to be close to home in case she needs me," I whisper.

"I'll get us back in time." Gene puts his arm around me and pulls me in closer to his chest.

"Okay one more minute, let me try Jenna again. If I can get her on the phone, I can convince her to join us." Cici is already punching in the numbers on her screen.

I roll my eyes. Cue the episode, The Waltons Go Gambling. Are we ever going to get out of this car?

The windows are fogging up inside, and outside it's freezing rain. No one's paying much attention to the weather, though, since we've just explained to Jenna how she got here and my relationship with the guy who made all that purple smoke.

"You screwed a genie? Like, the magical dude from a bottle?" Jenna has an incredulous tone at first, but then she bursts into laughter. "Mom, isn't that a little desperate? Even for you?"

Gene looks down at his lap, mortified. He can't look in her eyes after that comment. Not quite the reaction I expected. I thought she'd at least shake his hand.

"Jenna, I know it's hard to believe, or take seriously, but," I take Gene's hand in mine, "he's just like any other guy. Only, he happens to have magic in him, too. Please give him a chance."

Jenna stares at Gene for a few seconds, biting her lower lip. "Do you love her?"

"I do. A whole lot. She's wonderful. But, she's your Mom, so, you already know that." He looks up at her briefly, then glances away, out his window.

"Well okay, then," Jenna says. "Just take care of her. Can we go gambling, now?"

My girls have always believed in magic; especially in the pack of fairies living in our back garden, but they're older, now. Cynical. I thought this would be a whole lot harder to explain to them. I guess they really do want me to be happy.

"This town is gonna be sorry they let us in," Gram says. "I got money, but let's go make a shitload more."

Gene takes Gram's hand and helps her out of the limo first, then Jenna, Cici, and me. As I step out, my foot lands in a large slush puddle. There's a lot more snow piled up around us than I ever expected for Las Vegas. I can even see my breath surfing through the cold evening air. This is weird. Isn't Vegas supposed to be much warmer than Ontario?

Gram walks ahead of us all, and I do my best not to mother her and grab her arm. This freezing rain is making me nervous. Gene walks behind Gram, seemingly unaware of the rest of us. I know he's prepared, in case she slips. A young door man notices Gram's slow gait, rushes down the red carpeted stairs, and offers her his arm. She takes it, but stands straight, shoulders back, her pride intact.

"Thanks, dear," she says to the young man. "Couldn't keep your hands off me, I suppose."

"Sure couldn't." He beams.

She's starting to draw a small crowd of fans, and she knows

it. She makes the young man stop a minute before he opens the hotel lobby door for her, and turns to the crowd.

"On cold days like this, I put those hand warmers under my ass cheeks. They do things to me some men never could." Everyone bursts out laughing. The 20-somethings grab their selfie sticks, the 40-somethings hold up their phones, and those closer to Gram's age are waving pieces of paper. It's pandemonium. I want to protect her tonight, but Gene beats me to it.

"Folks, Bad Ass Grandma's going gambling, okay? She needs to save her energy. She can sign those another day."

"Oh, for God's sake, I can sign a few papers first." Gram motions for the group of onlookers to follow her into the hotel lobby and lets the young man take her coat. "You'd think I were an invalid the way you treat me! I still have life in me, yet," she says to no one in particular, but I know it's meant for me.

We all follow Gram into the lobby. People are coming and going in all types of attire, from mink coats and glittery gowns to low-rise jeans with a thong peeking out the back. We can't help but notice a young girl bending over a lobby coffee table, her thong completely exposed at the top of her jeans. Gram looks up at Jenna.

"If I were a young girl today, I'd be so confused. We sell 'em low rise jeans and butt floss underwear, but don't dare say vagina on TV."

Jenna laughs and nods in agreement.

Once Gram is settled in a chair signing autographs and taking selfies with her fans, the rest of us give our coats to the men and women in red uniforms who come forward for them.

The lobby is quiet for a moment. Cici and the girls are staring at the beautiful white statues at the center.

I'm staring at the sign that says Caesars Windsor. Not

Wynn. Windsor!

I'm not slamming Windsor. It's a pretty city, on a river, right across from Detroit. I see a signed, framed photo of Billy Joel on the wall beside the marble check-in counter. That's nice. Billy Joel has been here.

But I'd rather see him at Wynn, Las Vegas, thank you very much!

"Gene! We aren't..."

"Yeah, I noticed that a few moments ago." He sighs, flops down on a white leather sofa, and puts his feet up on the matching white ottoman. "I kinda fucked up again, didn't I?"

"Oh, Gene." I sit down beside him and notice Cici is at the marble counter with Jenna, already checking us in. "Never mind. This is Cici's wish, and she hasn't even noticed. Or if she has, she's not complaining. She's looking for a night of riches. This will do. I just hope she learns money can't buy happiness."

"You think? It bought your Wii, and your fancy phone, which brought me to you, which..." he smiles at me. "...brought you happiness."

"Oh, you think you bring me happiness, do you?" I take off my heels, which are already killing my feet, and turn toward him.

"Except for the times when I screw up, I think I bring you happiness. And I've been wondering Katherine, maybe, if..."

Jenna rushes toward us, gesturing excitedly. "You should see the rooms Cici booked for us. Executive suites. Adjoining rooms. They're amazing! So when we get tired of gambling, we can go on in and rest, whenever we want. This is so much better than studying for biology!"

"I hope the test isn't tomorrow, Jen." I try to sound calm and cool. "Not that it's my business; it's totally your life."

"Yes Mom, it's next week. I have lots of time." She looks

at Gene's hand on my knee. "Did I interrupt something, here?"

"Nope." I get up and slip my heels back on. "Can you go get Gram? I'm sure she could use a break from her adoring fans."

"Sure." Jenna looks over to where Gram had gathered a crowd around her, and we do the same. Only, Gram isn't there. I stand up and take a good look around the Augustus Lobby. She's not even in here, anymore!

"Uh, you want to text her?" Jenna asks with a chuckle. "It'd be better than shouting 'Grammie!' above the noise of the slot machines!"

"Give us a minute, we'll find her." Gene takes Jenna's phone from her outstretched palm, gets up, and heads for the casino doors. "If you lose me in the crowd, text Jenna's phone," he says over his shoulder.

Cici follows him, scrolling down the messages on her phone. I'm certain with her texting addiction, she's already sent out a couple texts to Gram, but Gram's phone is probably turned off. Jenna and I follow them through the doors, into the noisy chaos of the casino.

Chapter Ten

Lights flash and bells ding as we pass by people playing the slot machines. They look tired and somewhat bored, pulling at the levers like they're farmers pulling cows' teats for the ten-thousandth time. Over in the center of the room, people are gathered around games' tables. Cocktail waitresses, carrying trays full of drinks or empty glasses, are making their way through the lively crowd.

Gram's only been gone about a half hour. I can't imagine her being at one of those tables already, but Gene seems to think otherwise. He's walking rather fast, glancing back at me with a concerned look on his face. He appears to have spotted Gram at a table ahead of us. A stern-faced boxman is seated near Gram, managing the chips. Two grim-faced base dealers in expensive suits stand to either side of the boxman. They're collecting and paying bets to players around their half of the table. A less stern-faced stickman, also in an expensive-looking suit, has just announced the results of the last roll. He's moving the dice across the layout with an elongated wooden stick.

I quicken my pace and gesture for Jenna to do the same. We reach Gene's side as the crowd gathers a communal intake of breath. It's near-silence. Gram rubs her hands together, blows on them, and lets a pair of bright orange dice fly. They fly, fly fly... and the crowd roars. Some people applaud. Gram grins and takes a little bow. She glances my way and waves at us, licks her lips, blows on her hands, rubs them together, and calls out, "Show me the moneeeeee!" before rolling the orange dice again.

"Holy crap, Gene, Gram's playing craps! I don't think she's played before. I doubt she even knows how!" I call over to him, a little too loud. Everyone at the table turns their heads my way. The stern-faced boxman frowns at me. I turn away from the table and give Gene a look. He knows the one. It means, "A little help, here!"

Gene cups his hand over his mouth and tries to direct his voice into my ear. Making our conversation more private is close to impossible at this table.

"Craps is a game of chance, rather than skill. It has a low house advantage – around one point four percent – which makes it harder to beat than blackjack, but easier than roulette. Even novices can win. That is, if they're lucky."

"Lucky? So you're involved in this? Are you working your magic here, Gene?"

"I guarantee, Bae," Gene gives up shouting directly in my ear, "I have nothing to do with this. Cici wished to win the two million dollars, remember? Not Gram. She's doing rather well, though, from the looks of it."

"Uh, Gene?" I shout above the noise, not caring who hears. "What's with calling me Bae? I like Petal!"

"Just trying to keep up with the times, y'know," Gene shouts back. "I've been living in Greek times too long, thought I'd work on the *Lin-go* a little. Hey we could even take a selfie *right now* if you want." He takes Jenna's phone from his pocket, holds it up, and smiles his adorable awkward smile, the one he uses when he's trying to come across as cool and fails miserably.

"Gene, don't ever call me Bae again. It's a Danish word for poop."

Gene laughs and raises his hand like a white flag. "All right. Point taken. You'll never hear it from me again, Petal." He's so sexy when he doesn't try to be right, or even remotely from this century. I move in for a selfie and cuddle into the left side of his chest. We have to stretch a little to fit Gram furiously rolling her orange dice behind us, but we get the shot. As we check it out, it makes us both grin in silence.

I turn back to the craps table. Everything is moving so fast. The mood is frantic. People are yelling, "Yo!" at Gram. I can't keep up with the terminology, but I do remember the basics of the game.

"Okay, I know that she has to keep rolling her point number, which is eight, until she rolls a seven. When she rolls a seven, her turn ends. But, why are people yelling Yo?"

"That's the Yo eleven bet," Gene shouts. "It's one of the greatest wagers in all of gambling." He plays with the stubble on his chin, his once-concerned grimace turning into a wider grin with every roll of Gram's dice. He's totally sucked into this show. It probably feels good for him to watch something magical taking place for once, instead of him being at the center of the magic. Meanwhile, I'm about to lose my mind. My grandmother has a lot of money thanks to her hard work on her hit reality show. It's her money, not mine, but still, I don't want her to lose it all in one night.

A tall, thin brunette in a short red skirt walks up to us and offers complimentary drinks. "Tanqueray and tonic?" she asks with a smile. I look over at Cici and Jenna at the other side of the table, who already have their drinks in hand, and are raising them in celebration our way. I shrug my shoulders and take a drink off the tray. Gene doesn't take one. He's concentrating. He's watching Gram's every move.

Three and a half hours have passed, and three complimentary drinks later, Gram's still winning big. A larger crowd has gathered around our table. I'm not nervous for Gram anymore, thanks to those smooth gin and tonics. I celebrate with her every time she rolls an eight by high-fiving Gene.

"Holy craps! I did it again!" Gram yells, raises her arms high above her head, and swivels her hips in a full circle. "I'm on fire! Oh yeah, baby, oh yeah!"

The crowd roars with laughter.

"You go girl!" Cici and Jenna holler and pump their fists in the air.

"That's one hundred and fifty-three consecutive rolls," someone mutters. "She's already beaten The Captain's record!"

"She's headed for Guinness, if she keeps at it like this," a man in a yellow bow tie replies. "Just two more rolls!"

"Gram! Gram! Gram!" the people chant.

Gram's on her 156th roll. This is incredible to watch! Her face is glowing. She's really needed this lift since her show was cancelled. It's like she's in her own private reality show again, and I'm so thankful. It's just what the doctor ordered. Such perfect medicine. Too perfect. Wait a second...

Gram rolls a seven, and the crowd groans, then immediately bursts into applause.

"So, it's over. But what a streak! What a game!" the man in the yellow bow tie exclaims. He notices that he's got my attention. All other eyes are on Gram, who's downing a gin and tonic and high-fiving everyone in the crowd. The man continues talking to me in a monotone drawl.

"Given the rules of the game, there are any number of ways to achieve one hundred and fifty-five consecutive rolls without crapping out, though, all of them are highly unlikely." He fiddles with his bow tie, then continues, "Unlikely, but not impossible. However, I'd say there is a greater chance of being struck by lightning."

"Struck by lightning? Gene. Gene! I need to talk to you!" I look around for him, but he's nowhere close. I feel a vibrating motion from inside my little black purse. Pulling out my cell, I read the weirdest text I've ever received from my daughter. Ever.

<Bed completely unbroken. Get up here fast. ☺ >

Weird, until I realize it's Gene using Jenna's cell. Damn it, we have to get him his own!

"Excuse me," I say to the man in the yellow bow tie, "I have to go." I call across the table, and get a happy nod from my sister. "Cici! Stay with Jenna and Gram!"

As I head toward the casino exit doors and press the elevator button, I can already feel his skin on mine. I let out a low moan in anticipation as the doors close.

Gene's at the elevator door when it opens. He comes right in, scoops me up, and carries me to our room, kicking the door closed once we're inside.

I rip off his bowtie and start unbuttoning his shirt, and he throws me onto the King-size, pristine white bed. I bounce a little as I land on my back, dress hiked up to my hips, black stilettos in the air.

"Let's not break it yet, we need it first." I chuckle and kick off my shoes, but he's not laughing. He's not even coming up for air.

Chapter Eleven

The strong spray of hot water on my back relaxes my muscles – not that I need much relaxing after the last forty minutes with Gene. I lean my forehead against the shower wall and let the water run all the way down my neck and shoulders. I'm completely lost in the steam and heat until I feel a soft pair of lips kissing the nape of my neck.

"Hey, can a woman get clean, here? Gene! You've turned the water down to lukewarm."

"Can you blame me? You're already way too hot," Gene says and turns me around to face him. "Besides, I like it lukewarm in the shower."

"No, seriously." I give him the kind of peck married people offer when they're in a rush. "They could interrupt us any minute. We need to get showered and dressed."

Gene takes the shower gel and a pink bath poof, pours the gel on, and squeezes, creating a massive amount of suds. "Well, in that case, let me get you spic and span." He smirks and starts lathering my breasts and tummy.

I let him. It's too good to pass up. Leaning against the shower, I try to relax. We're alone. Together. Let go and enjoy, Cat! But, no. I can't. There are too many questions running through my mind about the last 12 hours.

"It was you, wasn't it? Gram's winnings? Before I left, I overheard she's won two-point-two million, Gene. That's what Cici wished for!"

"Yes." Gene bends down and scrubs the back of my calves. It tickles, but I try not to giggle. "Honestly, though, Cat, I didn't see it coming. It's the way Cici made her wish that let Gram take the winnings. I figured it out myself in the elevator as I was coming up here. Do you remember Cici's exact words?"

"She wished to take home two million."

"Right. Take home. She didn't specify that she should be the one to win it, only that we'd be taking home two million."

"And Gram's winning streak?" I grab the soap and start washing his back. The water is spraying across his broad shoulders, and I gently rub them. It's not easy, but I try to avoid rubbing his lower back because I know where that will take us. Instead, I concentrate on what I'm saying. "I heard from a craps expert that it's as likely as being struck by lightning. You can't say you weren't a part of that!"

"So, I gave her a little adventure. I've gotten to know your Gram pretty well. It's what she needed."

"Yeah, well, she's never satiated. You give her a little..."

"That sounds a lot like someone else I know." He turns around and kisses me hard on the lips. I drop the soap and move closer, letting myself get lost in the steam, the heat, and his body. I start to lift my leg and place one foot against the shower wall. My foot slips a little and leaves a curvy path all the way down the steamy glass.

"Cat, I want to ask you something, but we should probably get dressed for it." Gene stops kissing me and looks into my eyes.

"Cat! Get out here!" I see the back of Cici's head through the crack of the bathroom door. She's pacing across our suite's living room area.

"Ack!" I scream, opening the shower door and grabbing a towel off the rack. "How did you get in here? And why are you interrupting us, again?"

"I had front desk let us in. It's an emergency!"

"Us?" I ignore the emergency part for a minute and throw Gene a towel. "Is Jenna here?"

"Hi Mom," Jenna calls from the other room. "Having a good time?"

"Jenna! Oh, Fuckity. I'm so sorry everyone."

"There's no reason to be sorry, Katherine, it's our room." Gene wraps my towel tighter around me and gives me a squeeze at the hips.

I twist a second towel into a turban around my hair, make sure Gene's all covered, and rush out of the bathroom, through the bedroom, and into the suite's sitting room. I don't have time to be embarrassed anymore: something's up. From the look on Jenna's face, it's serious. Normally, she'd still be mocking me and Gene about our state of undress. Instead, she's biting her thumbnail.

"It's Gram isn't it?" I can feel it right away. I motion with a wave of my hand for Cici and Jenna to turn around, then grab my dress and shoes off the floor. I can see Gene is taking advantage of the ladies' turned bodies, and he's doing the same, only, he's taking precautions and pulling off his towel in the bedroom. Through the crack of the French doors, I can see him collecting the clothes we'd strewn across the room.

As I pull my dress over my head, I glance over at my sister and daughter. Cici's in her coat and boots; Jenna's dressed the same way. What the hell is going on?

"Cat, Gram wanted to leave. She was being hounded by paparazzi. We figured you two were... busy. So we started to head for the airport, and she slipped on the ice. She's badly hurt. Looks like a broken hip."

I sit down on the sofa and catch my breath. Jenna immediately sits beside me and takes my hand. "Mom, she's tough. Really. She'll be fine. She was conscious when they took her in the ambulance."

"Ambulance! Are you two nuts? We're in another city, in case you hadn't noticed! We should be back home! Plus, she's all alone in the back of that thing? Not good!"

"Actually she isn't alone," Cici answers. "One of the casino managers was kind enough to join her."

I buckle my shoes as fast as I can and get up. Gene's dressed, but his bow tie's shoved in his right pocket. I push it in further so it won't fall out and tuck in his shirt at the back. Jenna walks over to the coffee table and picks up her phone. I hope Gene deleted his sexy text to me. Oh well, no time to worry about that, now.

"Gene, you need to help us, here. We need to get Gram to our own hospital in Ottawa, and we need to get her healed."

Cici walks up to Gene and takes his hands. "Of course! I can't believe this didn't occur to me sooner. We'll wish Gram back to health. But this time, Gene, try to get us to the Ottawa Civic, not some hospital in Kathmandu." She chuckles. Obviously, she knew all along we weren't in Vegas and went with it.

"Sorry about the mix up, er, mix-ups, Cici. But you need to listen..."

Cici doesn't let him continue. "Oh Gene, we still had fun, and Gram will share her winnings with me, it's all good. Just, let's not screw up getting Gram well again."

I feel a wash of relief come over me as I realize Gram is going to be fine, thanks to Gene and his magic.

"Take us and Gram to the Ottawa Civic Hospital where she'll be immediately healed!" Cici holds Gene's hands tight as she says the words.

Gene opens his mouth a little and looks over at me with those beautiful, bright, pleading eyes again. I feel overcome with remorse, knowing I can't do anything to help him. He's grown so tired of this scene.

He hesitates, then says, "Your wish is my command!"

The hotel room starts tremoring like the ground in an earthquake. Tables, chairs, the sofa, and our bodies shake as purple smoke rises from the ground, first enveloping Cici and Gene, and then me and Jenna as we tightly hold onto each other. Jenna's face has turned white. She's freaking out.

"You do this often, Mom?" she shouts above the rattling noises. "This is your idea of fun times since I left home?"

I can barely see her eyes through the haze of purple smoke, but from what I can make out, she's not enjoying this as much as she used to enjoy our Ferris wheel rides.

"It's the best!" I squeeze her hands and give her a quick wink. "Jenna, it's all going to be okay. Trust me!"

A green vase falls off the bookshelf with a high-pitched crashing sound, shattering into a million tiny pieces. I close my eyes and pray I'm telling my eldest daughter the truth.

Chapter Twelve

Monday, February 20, 2017

2 a.m.

I wake up on a cold, hard, tiled floor, still holding Jenna's hand. She's shaking her head and looking around. I stand up and pull her up off the floor. People are staring.

Taking a quick look around, I realize we're in the triage waiting room. At least two-dozen people are sitting on hard, white plastic chairs. There's a woman knitting, a man in a surgical face mask hacking and coughing his head off, and a man in the corner of the room who looks like he's come in off the street. He's in a tattered green coat and an orange wool hat with pom poms on either side.

I look closer. Is he…? Seriously? Yes. He's mumbling to himself as he rips out pieces of the Yellow Pages from the phone book that's hanging off the pay phone on the wall. Rip. Rip. Riiiiiiip. Now he's taking his lighter and lighting the paper on the floor.

He's making a fire on the waiting room floor, and no one seems to notice!

"Excuse me! Uh! Fire! Fire!"

I shout and point at the growing flames. Everyone stops staring at me and Jenna, and instead avert their eyes to the man in the corner. A nurse rushes over and stomps all over the man's Yellow-Page fire. A couple people get up off their chairs and do the same, but they start coughing from the smoke. No one comes to take the man away. He simply sits back down on the floor and starts whittling a branch. This is the most ridiculous waiting room I've ever seen.

Once the fire is out, and everyone is back in their seats, I walk up to the counter and ask where to find Kate Morgan. Thankfully, we're quickly taken by a nurse to Gram's recovery room.

Gram has a big blue bruise on her forehead, an IV in her arm, and a tube up her nose for oxygen. I gasp and nearly faint when I see her looking like that, but the attending doctor tells me nothing was broken, and she can leave after some painkillers and a good night's sleep. I heave a sigh of relief when Gram sleepily opens her eyes to acknowledge me and Jenna with a nod.

Did she actually break a hip? Did the wish reverse her injury? I'll have to ask Gene. I put my purse on the chair next to the bed, kick off my heels, and turn to the door, where I think I'll find Gene and Cici standing against the door frame. They aren't there.

Jenna notices my look of concern. "Mom, they're probably getting us coffee. I'm sure they arrived here with us."

Something doesn't feel right. Gene should be here. So should my sister. Did they not make it into this wish at the same time as us? What's the delay?

"Gram," I take her hand, "you've been in an accident, do you remember?"

"For fuck's sake Cat, I'm old, but I'm not senile! Yes, I damn well remember. My ass remembers! My hip remembers! Everything hurts like hell!" She presses the little button on the remote beside her bed. The nurse has explained that it delivers timed pain medication.

I bend to kiss Gram on the cheek. "Alright, you sound like your usual self, but the doctor says you need to rest. The painkillers should kick in, soon. I'm going to go look for Cici and Gene and leave Jenna here with you for a while, okay?"

Gram nods, frowns at the morphine button and presses it one more time, then closes her eyes. I feel so relieved the wish worked. A 94-year-old with a broken hip is not a good situation. My 94-year-old Tell-it-like-it-is Gram with a broken hip? Recipe for disaster!

I walk across the hall and take an elevator down to the triage waiting room, where I expect I'll find Gene looking for me, too. It's that sixth sense of ours. It only took about four years for it to kick in. I smirk at my own joke and start humming along to the cheesy 70's elevator music.

As I leave the elevator, I can hear a whirlwind of activity at the sliding glass ER entrance doors. Two paramedics are rushing in with a patient on a gurney. Just as I get my bearings off the elevator, I lose them again. I do a double take, but continue stepping forward. My eyes feel like they're deceiving me. Am I really seeing this?

Cici and Gene are running inside the ER behind the gurney. Cici's face is frantic, and tears are streaming down her cheeks. Gene's expression is grim. He sees me and rushes over immediately.

"Cici got a text. She's next of kin. Your phone was off." He takes a breath and touches my shoulder before saying, "It's Alyssa."

"Alyssa? Oh, God! Did she slip on the ice, too?" I can't believe this. Not both of them in one night! I brace myself for what I'm about to see and begin to walk toward the commotion.

Gene grabs my arm and pulls me back. "No, it was something... else. Cat. I wouldn't look or listen right now, sweetheart." He envelops me in his arms, covering my face with his chest. "She's acting strange, and no one is sure why, yet."

It's too late. I can see from the corner of one eye. Alyssa is lying on the gurney, waving her arms wildly over her head. She looks over at me. Maybe if I meet her eyes, she'll calm down. I'm her mother; I can help. I know it.

Our eyes meet, and she starts screaming at me, and flailing her arms even more.

"You! You! You're one of them!" She's hysterical. I don't recognize her. She turns to scream at a paramedic.

"Get that woman over there! She's one of the One Direction groupies! They're everywhere! They're evil zombies! They're the One Direction Undead, and they're coming for us!"

I need to grab Gene to balance myself. Normally, Alyssa's the one making fun of people muttering nonsense to themselves at malls or in public washrooms. Okay, we don't actually make fun, that would be cruel, but we certainly give each other a Look.

Now, I'm giving Lyssa the Look. I'm wondering why she's going on about her most not-favorite boy band from her teen years. I have to give it to her, her delusions are fantastic. One Direction Zombies? This could be an SNL spoof.

I'm not amused like I usually am by her creative mind, though. I'm breathless, frightened, and confused. Her eyes are dark and glassy. Is my girl even in there, anymore? What the hell is going on?

"Get her!" She's still raging at me, pointing and practically foaming at the mouth. "She's the spawn of the devil, One Direction!"

One of the paramedics starts to reach for Alyssa's arms to pin them down. The other paramedic goes for her feet.

"Ow, oh fuck my chest! My chest! My chest hurts, and I can't breathe, Mommy!" She looks right at me. She sees me. Thank goodness, she knows I'm here. "Mommy, help me!"

My heart is breaking. I think I felt it literally break in half. This can't be good for my heart, but I can't help it. That's my little girl over there, and my hands are tied. There's nothing I can do to ease her pain.

The paramedics start rolling the gurney down the hallway where they're met by some nurses. As my daughter is wheeled away from me I wonder if I'll ever see her again. The room starts spinning. I need to sit down.

As they roll Alyssa into another room, I hear the tall, curly-haired paramedic talking to the blonde one. "She's a Goth girl. I'm sure she's messed up on Meth."

"Don't you dare talk about her like that!" I scream at him at the top of my lungs. "Don't you dare make assumptions based on her appearance! You know nothing about her! Nothing!"

Everyone in the triage waiting room stops and stares at me. I don't give a shit! They can't talk about her like that. I lunge toward the curly-haired paramedic, but Gene holds me back.

"Cat, I get it, but try to hold that stuff in. We don't want you arrested. Alyssa needs you right now."

Cici walks over and gives me a hug. I try to hug back, but I feel like I'm not even in my body, anymore.

"What happened? What just happened?" I cry into her shoulder.

"I don't know, honey, but she's in good hands here."

"They'll call us over to her soon, right?" I pull away from her. I feel so restless. "I need to talk to someone! I need to find out what's going on with her."

"I registered her. They know we're all here. They'll come get us."

"Jenna's with Gram..." I realize I should go get her, but I don't want to miss my chance to see Alyssa.

"We'll take care of everything," Gene says. "Why don't you sit down a minute, and one of us will go explain everything to Jenna."

Chapter Thirteen

Monday, 10 a.m.

The wait to speak to someone takes hours. I think I'm going to lose my mind.

Gene keeps bringing me coffee, and Cici tries to get me to play Angry Birds on our phones. I'm not in the mood. I stare into space, afraid I'm going to vomit all over the waiting room from worry. It doesn't help that Fire Freak is still in the corner, ripping out Yellow Pages from the phone book, and flicking his lighter whenever the nurses aren't looking his way. I'm going to die in a freak hospital fire set by some peanut butter nut bar, and I'll never see my daughter again. I start to hyperventilate and look around for a brown bag, but then I hear my name being called.

The doctor is handsome, young, and kind. He speaks in a hushed voice.

"We did bloodwork, x-rays, an EKG, and took a urine sample. These things do have a delayed reaction. When was the last time she used?" he says, looking down at a chart.

"Used?" I utter in disbelief.

"Meth. We found it in her system along with cannabis. Her chest pains were caused by costochondritis, an inflammation of one of her front rib joints. It can be caused by coughing and panic attacks, among other things."

"A panic attack? So, she didn't just suffer from a heart attack out there?" I ask.

"No, the meth intensified her anxiety, hallucinations, and panic. It's called Amphetamine Psychosis. It caused the increase in heart rate, rapid breathing, and raised her body temperature, which could have caused her to suffer from a heart attack or stroke, but she didn't. She's lucky. This time.

"She's going to feel strange for a few days, but then she'll be fine. She can stay tonight. We gave her some medicine to relax her and to control her breathing and heart rate.

I suggest that you check her into rehab as soon as possible, however." He hands me a pamphlet. Rideauview Rehabilitation. I remember seeing that sign on a two-story grey building when I was downtown once. I feel dizzy.

"The twenty-one day program should work best. Your family can get counseling, too."

"Psychosis? Rehab? Counseling? My daughter does not have a drug problem! This is a mistake!"

"Ma'am, I'm sorry to have to say this, but that's what all

the parents say." He gives me a strange, sideways smile, and leaves. I toss the pamphlet on a nearby chair.

I'm all alone with my sleeping daughter, and in this moment, I truly feel alone. At first, I stand beside Alyssa's bed, but she feels so far away from me. I fall on my knees to the cold hard floor and grasp her hand in mine. My daughter is as pale as a dead body, and her breathing is frighteningly irregular.

You'd think I would want to kiss her face, her forehead. You'd think I would want to stroke her hair and tell her how glad I am that she's alive. You'd think that. But I'm not just a mother, I'm a human being, and I can't be what society expects me to be in every situation.

In this situation, I'm going to be a raving lunatic.

"Lyssa, how dare you do this? How dare you! Are you stupid, or just selfish?" I raise my voice as loud as I can. She opens her eyes halfway and looks at me, but says nothing. "Okay, I married an asshole. Yes. I made some mistakes. But I fixed them. I fixed them! We've only just gotten our family back on track! You, me, Jenna. We're a team. You can't do this to us, now. You can't be messed up, just when I'm not!" I bury my face in the mattress and start sobbing.

I feel a hand on my shoulder. Gene is back. "Petal, you have to try to be calm. This isn't helping anyone. Especially you. Come here, let me hold you."

I stay on the floor, forehead against the mattress. I have no will left to move. I have a thought. "Maybe it was slipped to her. Maybe she didn't even know what she was smoking!"

He gives my shoulder a gentle squeeze. "I have no idea, and she's fallen asleep again. We'll have to wait until she wakes up. Then, we can talk to her, together, if you want. Although we'll have to explain about me and assure her I'm not a delusion."

I chuckle a little because I'm running out of tears.

"You should try to rest until then. You haven't slept all night. I'll go check on Gram and get a nurse to bring you a mattress for the floor," he says.

I keep my back to him, head down, my cheek against the soft blanket, until another idea comes to me. "You can fix this, right Gene? Cici can wish her better! She could wish this all away!"

I turn my head to see what he has to say, but he's already gone.

Monday, 5 p.m.

I open my eyes slowly and see Gene sitting cross-legged in the chair opposite me, reading the pamphlet I'd left there. I can't remember where I am, but this is the most uncomfortable mattress I've ever slept on. The room is dark; Gene gets up slowly, walks over to the window, and opens the shade.

"Hi. They said they'll be bringing Lyssa her meal soon, so I guess you should get up, too.

"Oh, while you were sleeping, she asked who I was. I kept it simple: we're good friends. We can explain more later."

As he raises the shade, low, evening sunlight fills the room. There's a slab of grey to the left and a parking lot to the right just outside the window. A uniformed woman, who looks to be in a bad mood and a great hurry, enters the room pushing a cart carrying trays of food. If you can call any of it food. All I can make out from here are the clear bowls of red Jell-O.

So, I am in the hospital. First Gram, then Alyssa. It wasn't all one big horrible nightmare. Crap.

I pull back the small brown blanket and sit up. I'm not sure if I'm shivering out of fear or the cold, but Gene notices and hands me my coat. I quickly pull it on over my little black dress.

"Jenna went to Lyssa's place and is packing her a suitcase," Gene explains. "Just in case..."

"In case we need to put her in that place?" I gesture with my head to the pamphlet in his hand and stand up.

Alyssa is awake, sitting up in bed. I guess a nurse gave her her purse because she's reapplied her black lipstick, and it looks like someone combed her newly blue highlighted, jet-black hair. She's picking at her plate of food with a fork, but not eating anything.

"I don't believe it. I can't believe it..." My right eye is twitching. I bite my lower lip.

"You can call it what it is, Mom. Rehab," Alyssa grumbles, lifting the lid on her red Jell-O container. "Ick. Jell-O. Fuck My Life!"

That's it. Enough. Enough of all of this.

"Alyssa." I stomp over to her bed and push her tray away before one of us throws it. "I hate that expression. I fucking hate it, okay? First off, your life was pretty damned fantastic except for your drunken dad, which I've apologized for profusely. But you didn't seem to accept the apology. What is this..." I lift my arms out and gesture around the room, "are you getting back at me?"

"I dunno. Dad gave it to me."

"Jimmy? Jimmy gave you what?"

"He gave me the pot one night, when he came by to see me. He hung out with me and my friends a while. I thought it was just pot, but it turns out... well, we all got a little higher than usual... and then they wanted more..."

"That bastard! I want to rip him to shreds!" I shout and turn to Gene, tears pouring out of my eyes. I'm unable to contain my sadness and my rage.

"Since when did you call Jimmy your dad, Alyssa?" Cici's standing at the door, her face aghast. She's there with Jenna, who's holding a small black duffel bag.

Alyssa bites her thumbnail and looks down at her hands in her lap. "I dunno. My friends called him that, and I... I wanted to have a dad for once, okay? For once in my life!"

"Well, Lyssa, you don't have a dad," I say. "He's an abusive shit who contributed genetic material to make you, but he's no dad. Why did you even let him into your place? What the hell?"

"I... told you... my friends let him in. They don't know about my childhood."

I sit down on her bed and wipe my left cheek. The tears are still coming. I can't stop them. I can't ease her pain, and I'm starting to feel numb from mine. "How long have you been doing this? This pot and meth thing?"

Alyssa takes a deep breath and is silent for a minute before speaking. "It was just pot for a while."

"Just pot? Just? Just?" Jenna is livid. She tosses aside the duffel bag and glares at her sister. "Lyssa, do you know what that crap does to your brain? And the dealers, they put all kinds of other shit in there to get you hooked. Like crystals!"

"I know, now, okay? Geezus Fuck. I know, now! I just didn't know it, then. We all liked that it was a greater high. So, I got more from Dad a few weekends later, and then this weekend. It was all free..."

"That's it." Gene steps in closer so he can look at both me and Lyssa. "I'm calling the police. We need to press charges."

Cici puts her hand on Gene's arm. "It's okay. Cat, sweetie, don't worry about this. I'll make the call. That bastard's going to be looking at some serious time."

Lyssa starts to sob. "But it's... Dad. I mean, it's my dad!"

I try to take her hand, but she pushes it away. She's inconsolable.

I'm not sure I'm in my own body. I can't control the emotion pouring out of me, and my brain feels like it's misfiring every piece of information. I stay sitting on the hospital bed, but look up at Gene with pleading eyes.

"Gene, sweetheart, please, please, give Cici her last wish. Cici," I look over at her. "Wish us out of this mess!"

Gene sits on the bed beside me and takes my hand in his. "Katherine. I've been trying to tell you this for a while. You... all of you, I think, you've lost track of the wishes..." He lowers his voice to a near-whisper.

"There are none left. I-I know this is bad timing, but I guess it's kinda good news? Cici freed me with that last wish that helped Gram."

I wipe my nose on my sleeve. This is so not how I imagined this moment. "You're free?"

"I am finally a free man." He squeezes my hand, lifts it, and kisses it. His eyes are misty.

"So, does that mean you're going home to your son?" There's a lump in my throat. I swallow hard to try to hold back the strong mix of emotions I'm feeling.

"That's what is supposed to happen, yes, in the next twelve hours. Or else..." He glances over his shoulder and out the door nervously.

"Or else what?"

"Maybe we should talk about this somewhere else." He gestures over at Jenna and Alyssa. Jenna has grabbed her sister's Jell-O off the tray and is eating it like a ravenous golden retriever. Cici is on her cell, probably with the cops, as promised.

She's covering one ear as she speaks into the phone, scrunching up her face so tight her brows are furrowed and her nose looks like a wrinkled prune. Her nose always does that when she's angry.

"Maybe, okay, but... Fuckity! I can't do any of this without you! I'm sorry, I don't know what will happen if you stay, but I need you to, Gene. You can't leave me, now. You just can't!" I can feel my hands shaking in his.

"Katherine. You are an amazing mother. The power of your love is worth a thousand wishes," he says. I feel my heart pounding fast inside my chest cavity. His words can't heal the damage done today, but they feel like the closest thing to real medicine.

"You can do this. And, I'll never leave you. Never. Think of it as a temporary absence."

It feels like he's looking far into my soul when he looks at me. I nearly get lost in his eyes for a moment, but then decide I need to know what he means by 'temporary absence.' Just as I start to ask, Gram walks in. She's moving with quite a lot of power; not even shuffling. She's dressed in her gold running shoes and velour dress and looks about ready to hit the craps table again. I'd say I can't believe my eyes, but I can. When Gene actually gets his magic right, it doesn't surprise me anymore.

"Alyssa Jane Glamour! What were you thinking? Or not thinking!" She puts her hands on her hips and glares at her youngest great-grand daughter.

"Gram. Go easy," I plead softly. "Have a seat. We're about to talk to her about... a serious decision."

"I'm. Not. Going." Alyssa's voice is firm as she lies back on her pillow, pulling the covers over her head.

"Young lady, you most certainly are!" Gram pulls the covers back off of Lyssa's body and gets right up in her face.

"Oh, Gram. I made such a big mistake." Alyssa starts sobbing, and I feel slightly hopeful. Where there is regret, possibly, there can be change.

Chapter Fourteen

Rideauview Rehab Centre – Day 15

March 7, 2017

As I pull up into the small parking lot and take my keys out of the ignition, I feel my stomach churning with nervousness. I never know what to expect from these visits.

The first week, Alyssa didn't even want to see me. I'd stand at her door, and she'd throw pillows and books at me, screaming,

"I told you I didn't want to be here! But you did this to me! You!"

Even as my heart split in two pieces, I stood there, smiling through the pain, and told her that I loved her. She kept throwing books at me until a couple staff members came in to restrain her and ushered me away from the room. I tried to look on the bright side: at least she didn't think I was a One Direction Zombie, anymore. The doctor said that her psychosis was finished, so I knew one thing for certain: she hated me for me.

It's been one of the most heartbreaking times of my life. I'd been a mother to this girl for 20 years, and she couldn't stand the sight of me. I wasn't sure where I belonged anymore, so I simply sat in the lobby every morning that first week, holding Gene's hand in silence. He told me before he'd have to leave, but he's still here, and I'm grateful for it.

Gene has been like a rock through all of this. He doesn't interfere with my parenting, or what I feel sometimes is a lack of parenting because I'm completely overwhelmed by the situation; he's just here, beside me when I need him.

He's even been sitting in on our family counseling sessions. The coordinator assumes we're a married couple, and I didn't feel like correcting him. Alyssa, knowing we're a couple, doesn't seem to care. In fact, in the beginning, she didn't care about anything. She wasn't even looking at or talking to anyone at first, so she didn't complain. When she finally started talking, it was mostly about Jimmy, and it often took most of the session to calm her down. Her anger lessened slightly when she learned Cici and Gene had the police raid Jimmy's home and found a grow-op in the basement.

Jimmy's being retained until sentencing in June, and is looking at over a decade in prison for possession and trafficking. The grow op? That will only get him six months for six plants, so, in his case, possibly a year. However, my lawyer says he will definitely do more time for the trafficking, possibly as long as

14 years.

Though he's behind bars, at least for now, I lose sleep at night worrying that he'll escape. All we can do is issue a restraining order against him, and hope the justice system will protect us once he's out. Alyssa and one of her smarter friends, Annabelle, have agreed to testify that he got them, and many of their friends, hooked on his products, so they wouldn't be charged with possession or social sharing.

I didn't think Gene would be allowed to stay with me this long, but I know he's doing it to help me and Alyssa. Is he even following The Rules genies are supposed to adhere to after granting three people their wishes? I know he's supposed to be home with his son, but I don't want to think about that. Every day that I get to wake up beside him is a bonus.

For the last few weeks, we've often slept the entire night on a purple, modern, horribly uncomfortable leather bench in the Rehab Centre lobby, so I can see Alyssa first thing in the morning, before our daily counseling session. The staff doesn't seem to mind, and they keep apologizing that there are no extra beds available for family members. When I do see Alyssa, she doesn't usually speak to me, but with every day, I notice slight improvement.

The other day, when we were alone, she asked me what it's like sleeping with a genie on a leather bench. "Was it as comfortable as his bottle?" she asked, her voice unwavering. I think, however, that I may have seen a smirk on her face.

There must be an art to bench-sleeping, and whatever it is, Gene and I haven't yet mastered it. This morning, I found Gene lying on the cold marble floor beside me. Snoring. It doesn't matter what he's sleeping on, he always manages to snore. At some point in the middle of the night, one of the staff members took pity on him and covered him in a wool blanket. I took one look at him, the big lump of blanket and bed head on the floor, and decided a hot breakfast was in order, so I headed out early to grab us some breakfast sandwiches at Timmies.

As I enter Rideauview with my take-out breakfast and tray of coffees, I scan the bright and welcoming lobby area for Gene. He isn't here. Why does he always disappear like this with no explanation? He did this at the hospital a few times, too. I don't want to keep a tight leash on the guy; he's been a prisoner of stasis long enough. I just wish he were better than me at answering texts. I guess it would help if he actually had a phone. He's always using Jenna's, Cici's, or even Gram's to reach me. Mental note: I need to get the guy a phone.

Well, we'll find each other again, soon. I told him I'd be heading to Alyssa's place this afternoon after spending a couple hours at the Centre. Alyssa should be returning home in less than five days, and I want to clean her place a little, make sure it looks welcoming for her return. Damn, I wish Cici and I still had wishes left! Maybe I'd wish Alyssa's place clean. Then I'd wish she stay clean and healthy for the rest of her life.

I know life has no guarantees, but these last few weeks, watching my daughter struggle with an addiction, have been pure hell from which I want a Guaranteed Way Out. Wishing it all away with a whirl of purple smoke from Mr. Magic would have been wonderful, but he was absolutely correct about the power of parental love. I've learned more by having to rely on myself and the love of Gene and my family. It's as cheesy as my fingers after eating Cheetos, but the Beatles were right: all you need is love.

Jimmy's going to prison, and Alyssa needs a few more weeks of counseling before the doctors feel she'll be in the clear. They suggest she take some time away from the so-called friends who steered her wrong. Funny, but I feel like the counseling has done me almost as much good as it's done Alyssa. It wasn't meant to address my weight issues, but it has.

Alison is our loveable but no-nonsense, silver-haired, 52-year-old family counselor at the Centre. She taught us that one of the key reasons kids turn to drugs is poor self-esteem. I immediately felt responsible for Alyssa's low self-esteem when I heard that, but she assured me there are a dozen reasons why Alyssa went through this stage of low confidence.

Then, she turned to me, gently took my hand, and said, "Don't you ever go through times when you feel inadequate, Cat? It's the same for teens and young adults. They just deal with it differently. Adults? We go buy a power suit, or a Ferrari."

I chuckled, and then I spilled. It was like a Volcano of Self-Loathing poured out from inside of me, having been simmering for years deep inside my soul. Alison and Alyssa listened to me for over an hour. There were tears, Kleenex, snot, and laughter. Yes, Alyssa even laughed out loud when I talked about Ledussa, my Godess of Self-Loathing.

"You gave her a name? A Greek name? Mom! How lame can you be?" But then she laughed – a good, long laugh from the belly – stretched out one leg, and kicked my running shoe a little. It was an affectionate kick. I could feel the love in that kick, but I tried to hide my elation, because I didn't want her to know how much that mattered. Not yet.

Alison gave me and Alyssa some tools for self-talk. She said women of all ages, but especially ones over 20 with jobs and responsibilities and families, despise feeling guilty. To avoid feelings of guilt, we satisfy the "haves" in our lives before we satisfy ourselves. She suggested we try taking words like "have," "must," "should", and "ought" out of our vocabularies – words that fill us with guilt and anxiety. She said we should help one another out with this technique – we need to call each other out if we hear ourselves using those words.

Alison also taught us that perfection does not exist. It's subjective. Women strive to be perfect, and then end up either having some kind of breakdown, or become frustrated by perceived failure, and give up on goal-setting altogether.

One day last week, Alison told us to strive for self-actualization instead of perfectionism. When she left the room a minute to take a private phone call, Alyssa surprised me with one of her best impressions yet.

"Let's *self-actua*lize, shall we, now?" she said, imitating Alison's British accent. "I don't know how to do it but let's just sit here and hum and *believe* in ourselves!" She handed me a mirror, held up one to her own face, and began making silly faces at it.

I chuckled, but then had to hush her quiet. I put the mirror down on the table beside me. "Shh, she could come back any second. Besides, she could be onto something. Only, I don't know what the hell self-actualization is, either. Should we ask her?"

Alyssa giggled. "It's more fun not knowing and mocking her, but okay."

My heart leapt. She's laughing. My baby is laughing. Not just with anyone: with me! I can breathe again. We're on our way.

I climb the stairs to Rideauview's second level, balancing a tray of lukewarm coffees in one hand, a bag of breakfast sandwiches, and my Monster Purse in another. As I open the heavy metal door, I hear laughter down the wide hallway. One of those is easy to recognize: Gram's mischievous chuckle is contagious! No way. Is that Alyssa joining her? This I have to see.

The door to Alyssa's small, light blue room is open, so I

walk inside and place the tray of coffees down on the tall dresser. Alyssa is sitting cross-legged on her bed, dressed in her baggy purple plaid PJ bottoms and a big white T-shirt. She's laughing at Gram, who's sitting in the leather chair at the end of the bed wearing a plastic headband with a game card that says "Ballerina."

"Hey, Mom," Alyssa's eyes are bright and shining, "we're playing Headbanz. It's this game we used to play all the time with Jenna, remember? Anyway, Gram is having trouble guessing who she's supposed to be, so I was thinking of demonstrating, but now that you're here..." She smiles at me like she actually likes me and takes the small black coffee and two creamers I hand her.

"Ah, and since when was I any good at drama?" I answer, but I twirl a couple times for Gram and raise my hands above my head. In the process, I lose my balance, and need to grab the dresser for support.

"You gotta pee, cupcake? Washroom's across the hall." Gram reaches for the bag of breakfast sandwiches, opens it, sticks her nose in, and takes a good long whiff.

"No, Gram," I chuckle. "I was acting. That was supposed to be what your headband says."

"And that's why I became the reality star and not you," she says, then bites into a warm English muffin.

"Alright, smart alec, let's see you do a better job with Lyssa's." I take off my coat and throw it over a chair, sit on the bed beside my daughter, open the tab on my coffee lid, and take a small sip.

I turn to read Alyssa's headband. It has the word "Zombie" on it. Holding my breath, I look at Gram. Lord, let Alyssa have a sense of humor about this. Is it too early? It could be too early! I don't know what to do, but Gram immediately takes control. She gives me a wink and gets up out of her chair. Walking like the undead, arms outstretched straight in front of her, with eyes wide, she shuffles right up to Alyssa, then sticks out her tongue to the side.

"Miley Cyrus?" Alyssa kids, then says as loud as she can, "You're a zombie!" She starts chuckling a little, seeming uncomfortable at first, but then her giggles spill into a deep guttural contagious laugh that has me nearly snorting. I have to put down my coffee so I don't spill it.

Lyssa reaches forward and hugs Gram tight, nearly pulling her over onto the bed. "Gram, that was bang-on! I almost thought you were a delusion!" She looks over at me; a wry look on her face.

"Hey, none of that, we're done with delusions. Done!" I walk forward slowly, wondering if I can join in the hug. I hesitate, then put an arm around each of them, and for the first time in weeks, Alyssa doesn't pull away.

"Group hug!" she mumbles into my shoulder. It's the best feeling in the world.

After a minute, Gram is the one who pulls away. "Enough mushy stuff, ladies, I want my breakfast, hot." She returns to her chair and continues munching away on her sandwich. Then, she reaches into the bag and throws a wrapped sandwich to Lyssa and one to me.

"Thanks, Gram." Lyssa unwraps her sandwich and takes a bite. "Mmm. So much better than the shit they serve here," she says.

"Hey, that shit is costing me a second mortgage," I joke.

"Seriously? God, Mom, I'm so sorry." Lyssa actually looks choked up.

"Oh honey, I was kidding, it's not that bad." I glance over at Gram. "Gram's helping. You know she's totally loaded, right?" We all start to giggle, but have to stop so we don't spit out our food.

"About that," Gram puts her food back on the wrapper and looks serious, "when you're all better, Lyssa, I want to take a family trip. I'm not gettin' any younger, and my money is just sitting in the bank, wasting time. 'Cause time is money. So I say let's spend my money on what really matters. Being together."

"Wow, Gram, that's very generous. I..." Alyssa pauses to gather her thoughts. "I think I am better. This place has been good for me. I think I'm finally becoming the person I want to be." Her voice starts to quiver and tears are streaming down her cheeks. She wipes them with the back of her pillow, squeezing it tight against her chest.

"I'm so sorry, Mom, Gram, I'm so sorry I made such a stupid mistake!"

"Hogwash. All the stupid mistakes I've made are also the best stories of my life." Gram gets up, sits down on the bed beside Lyssa, and starts rocking her in her arms, gently, like she did when she was a baby. "It's all part of what makes us human. We're human."

"Oh Gram, I certainly think I'll get a good story or two out of this mistake." Lyssa chuckles amid the tears, burying her face into Gram's chest. I sit down in my chair and watch my Lyssa rocking back and forth in Gram's strong, loving arms like she did 20 years ago, and the days, months, years melt away. I'm choked up, and badly in need of Kleenex, but I also can't help thinking that his would make one awesomely touching Tim Horton's commercial.

That is, until Gram opens her mouth again. "Hey, kid. It's alright to cry. Just don't get snot on my custom-Calvin Klein hoodie."

Chapter Fifteen

The minute I open the front door to Alyssa's apartment, a small, thin white cat that looks part Siamese and part tabby comes running up to me and wraps his body around my right leg like I'm his long-lost friend.

I know better than that. I know he just wants me because I can open a can of cat food.

"Mewwwww?"

"Yes, Marmie, you're hungry aren't you?

I give the little guy a chin rub, take off my boots and hang up my coat. The cat continues to rub against both my legs. His purring sounds like a toy motorboat. He's such a cute little kitten. I bet he misses his mommy, the poor fella...

Holy Hell! What the *fuck*?

I cannot believe what I'm seeing. I walk forward into Lyssa's tiny, patchouli-scented, red-and-brown coordinated living room, stop and have a good, long look at the brown pleather ottoman we bought together when she first moved in.

The ottoman looks like a Rottweiler decided it was its favorite chew toy of the day. It's not just slightly bitten. It has large-dog-mouth-sized chunks of pleather and stuffing pulled out of every corner. There are brown bits of fabric and white furniture stuffing strewn across the floor, and a couple of chewed-up cushions. A hailstorm from hell has descended upon this apartment. I don't know whether to laugh or cry. I turn to find Marmie cowering behind an aloe plant in the corner.

The cat ate the ottoman.

I don't even bother disciplining him. This cat clearly has some kind of eating disorder.

Bending down, I start picking up the pieces and realize I'm going to need a large garbage bag to gather everything. As I head to the kitchen to grab one from the cupboard under the sink, I hear someone knocking at the door. I look through the peep-hole and see Gene in a black-leather jacket and blue jeans, holding a couple of drinks in his hands.

"Hot chocolate?" he says and walks inside. He hands me my cup and starts to kiss me, but gets distracted when he sees the state of the living room from his peripheral vision.

"What happened here?"

"The cat happened. Marmie happened." I point to the small white feline, who's in his cozy cat bed by the sofa, giving himself a bath.

"Geesh, is it starving or something? I thought you and Cici were feeding it every day."

"We are. Maybe something's missing in his diet."

"Yeah, like the vitamins that come from cowgirl hats?" Gene's standing inside the doorway to Lyssa's bedroom, laughing and shaking his head. He's found Lyssa's favorite red cowgirl hat; the one she loves to wear on Canada Day. It has Marmie-sized bite holes all the way around the rim.

"That little shit! Give that to me!" I put down my hot chocolate, take the hat, and inspect it. It's ruined. I lunge toward the cat, but Gene grabs me at my shoulders.

"Seriously, it's a little too late to teach him a lesson. C'mon. I'll help you clean up the mess."

I sigh and throw the hat on the coffee table. "Okay, here, hold this bag for me," I say and start shoving fluff and brown pleather pieces inside it.

The living room looks almost presentable. Our empty hot chocolate cups are on the small table by the front door, along with two large, filled garbage bags. Lyssa's red hat is on the top of one of the bags. I'm wondering if Gram or Cici may have an idea as to how to repair it for Lyssa before she returns home.

As I start to clear off some junk that's been piled up on Lyssa's coffee table, Gene takes my hand and tries to get me to sit down on the sofa.

"We should talk."

I let go of his hand and keep clearing the coffee table. "If it's about the wedding, Gene, we don't have to do anything that—" I stop myself halfway through my sentence and look up at him. I'm not being truthful with myself. I need to be real with him if we're going to last.

After spending so much time with Gene lately, I know for sure that I do want the fairy-tale ending. I'm old-fashioned, and I know what I want. I want to be married to him and not keep messing about with time-traveling adventures! I love this man. In the end, I want him to be happy, too. I should go for a position of strength, but unselfishness.

"Look, I'll be fine. I know you were supposed to go home a while ago, home to your son, and you've somehow managed to put that off..."

Gene opens his mouth to interrupt, but gets distracted by the pile of eight or so seed packets on the kitchen counter. He walks over to them, picks one up, and starts reading the back.

"If sowing inside and planting outside, you can sow in late February," he reads the instructions aloud and gestures for me to come over.

So, I guess we're done with that other conversation. We both felt its awkwardness. How does someone gear up to tell you they're leaving you so they can be in another time with their son? Possibly forever? I don't want to talk about this right now. From the looks of it, neither does Gene.

"Hey," he says and gives me a quick little kiss on the lips, "I bet Lyssa was planning on growing this in pots out on her balcony. We should start some for her! They'd be seedlings by the time she comes home!" His voice is high-pitched. He seems excited and nervous. Is this just about the basil?

"Sow the seed thinly and if growing in pots sow enough for a few plants in each pot," he continues. "Cover with six millimeters of compost and press down gently. Basil seeds usually germinate in seven to fourteen days at temperatures around twenty-two degrees Celsius. Once established, basil needs very little care."

I stare up at him as he finishes reading the packet. I love how I learn something new about him every single day. I don't think it's because we've had little time to get to know each other; I think it's because there is so much to know about Gene. He's complex. He's got soul. I mean seriously, he's a genie in a black leather jacket, getting excited about seeds! I realize I've been holding my breath for what feels like three minutes. I exhale deeply and relax into him, placing my head against his chest.

"So, something's going on with you. There's got to be more to this than seeds."

"Sure. It's not just about seeds. Think of it as... a metaphor for the challenges we face in life. You. Me. Lyssa. Here, look at this." He takes the packet, rips it open, shakes out a tiny basil seed onto the palm of his hand, and holds it up toward the light.

"There's so much potential locked up inside this one little seed, but it can't germinate without being in a dark place first." He has tears in his eyes.

Seeing him emotional, in turn, makes me choke back tears.

"We've been in some dark places alright. My weight and depression. Our struggles to save Ben and Logan's lives. Being forced apart for so long, and lately, trying to help Lyssa find her light again." I open the bag of soil Alyssa had left on the floor beside the large pantry. There are three small red pots beside the soil, so I place them out on the kitchen counter, then start pouring the soil. Gene pats the soil down into each pot with the palm of his right hand.

"So we'll think of these seeds like symbols of our dreams. You can't realize the bright, shining goal without being in a dark place before that," he says,

My heart beats faster as I suddenly get his point, and continue his thought. "...without having to stretch for the light, to deal with adversity," I say as I plant small basil seeds inside the first pot.

"Exactly. The seed can't grow without it. I guess we can't either." He opens the watermelon and mint seeds packets and places those in the second and third pots. "But just wait. Just wait and see."

"Uh," I chuckle, "you want to grow watermelon out on the balcony? In Canada?"

"Why not? Nothing's impossible. We've proven that." He takes the pot of watermelon seeds, hands it to me, grabs the pot of herb seedlings, and places them on the kitchen windowsill. Then, he walks back to the living room. He seems so on edge. It doesn't appear possible for him to stand still today.

"We'll transplant the watermelon seedlings once they get too big for their pots," he calls to me. "We'll find a garden for them."

"We?" I hesitate. "So you're planning on staying the summer, then?" I join him in the living room.

"Uh," he glances out Alyssa's large, living room window. "I've been meaning to tell you. I want to. God, I want to more than anything, but, see..." he pulls Alyssa's red curtains further apart so he can see the street below us.

"Oh, buggerallfucknuts!" He turns away from the window, the color draining from his face. "He's found me. He's finally found me!" He jumps behind the curtain and is so dramatic about it, I wonder if there may be gunfire at any moment.

"Katherine, I really have to go. Now. I'm so, so sorry, and I promise I'll make this up to you! Lock the door. Stay safe." He kisses each of my eyebrows like it might be the last time and kisses me hard on the mouth. Then, he practically sprints through Alyssa's living room and out the front door.

"What the? Who's found you? Who?"

I'm left alone and completely baffled, standing beside a pile of black garbage bags and a half-eaten red cowgirl hat, holding a pot of potential.

"Mewww?" Marmie rubs vigorously against my right leg.

"Oh, you, Eater of Everything, you just shut up."

I grab my coat, take my potential and the bag of double-stuffed Oreos on the counter, and leave.

Chapter Sixteen

Seven weeks later

Saturday, April 29, 2017

"I am never wearing a thong on an airplane again. I've never been more uncomfortable in my life."

Gram shifts in her seat a little, pulling at the back of her black polyester pants, then groans in defeat and takes a swig of her drink.

"You'd think these people could learn to make a proper Whiskey Old-Fashioned, with all the free hours they've got up in the air," she grumbles, sweeping a strand of her long, snow white hair off of her face. "But I suppose they're too busy joining that Mile High Club." She carefully undoes her high hair bun, then resets it.

"Gram, this is a flight to Paris, not a nineteen twenties' bar, and the Mile High Club doesn't exist, anymore. I'm sure you're gravely disappointed." I chuckle, and close my novel. I wasn't enjoying it, anyway.

"Just because there are rules in place, doesn't mean people are following them. I've seen you texting and driving, Cat, don't try to deny it."

How does she know everything? Win at everything? I give up. I'd definitely lose at craps to her, but together, we'd win at charades. I take off my glasses, put them in their case, and tuck them inside my purse beside my boarding pass: Katherine Glamour, Seat 11B Flight 9011 Paris April 29, 2017. It's nestled beside one that reads Katherine Morgan 11A and another one behind that, Cecily Glamour 11C.

Alyssa has her own boarding pass and a seat right up front, the Princess. She got a first-class ticket from Jimmy for her recent birthday. What kind of parent gives such a large gift to one child, but not the other? Him. Jimmy. Jimmy pulls that kind of shit.

Only Jimmy would try that kind of trick from jail, the ass monkey. When the ticket arrived in Lyssa's birthday card, I didn't even wonder how he got access to money. It was his parents. They do everything for him. They would clean up his jail cell of vomit and dirty, five-day-old dishes for him if he asked.

Jenna was cool about it, though, since she couldn't take that much time off work, anyway. She plans to take the red-eye on the third and join us at our hotel.

After we all calmed down – just the thought of Jimmy

makes us all want to puke – I decided after all that Lyssa had been through, it would be wrong for me to make her return the ticket because I hate my ex's gloating guts. She deserves this first-class ticket, and more, for beating her addiction. At the time, though, when Gram suggested we all follow Alyssa and go to France together, I assumed Gram was getting the rest of us first-class tickets, too. The woman's a millionaire, and yet, she still watches her purse strings when it comes to travel. She booked us rooms in a swanky hotel, but oddly enough, insisted we fly using airline points. Points? Airport hassle? I'd kind of been hoping she'd book us a private jet.

"Gram, there's no chance you want to just charter us a, um, y'know, a private jet? It'd be so much comfier." I decided to be bold and ask her outright the morning we were booking the trip.

"Hell, no. If Prince William can fly commercial, so can we. What's the point of having all these Air Miles and never using them?" she said. "That's like wasting a perfectly good box of condoms."

I shook my head and pretended I hadn't heard that.

Except, when I lose my head over cute shoes and lingerie, I'm also frugal by nature. I would have waited another month to find a better deal, but we needed to arrive in Mornas by May 4th.

May 4th. I have so much riding on that date. Three months ago, I felt like I was waiting for that day for my life to begin. Now, I don't quite know what to expect when that day finally rolls around.

I can't believe I let Gram talk me into taking this trip to France, in hopes we find Gene waiting for me at the castle. Talk about setting yourself up for a major disappointment. I know he loves me, but there are so many obstacles in our way. For one, he's missing again. It's been seven weeks. Then, there's the minute factor that he doesn't even want to get married!

Spleroosh! Damn! My cranberry juice spilled out of the cup, all over my tray. Good. A flight attendant is coming to my aid… er, maybe not. He's cleaning up the tray and closing it.

"We're experiencing turbulence right now. You'll have to put this away, and please push your bags under the seat in front of you." He doesn't even smile at me. Or give me those yummy soft cookies. Now I'm irritated.

I glance over at Gram to see if she shares my annoyance. Remarkably, she's completely unruffled. She's staring at me with those shrewd, sky blue eyes, still waiting on my answer about texting and driving. Damn it! Ever since I was old enough to understand what fibbing was, I've been unable to lie to my Gram. She raised me well. She knows my every expression.

"Okay, you got me, Gram. I'll pull over next time I need to text while driving if you stop tweeting me from that disco you and Pat go to. It creeps me out to get woken up with a notification that you're 'Feeling the Funk.' I never know what to make of that!"

I wish Gene could send me a notification. I've tried everything short of smashing my phone against the wall to make him return.

I don't think it's a case of abandonment. He came back to me. Spent time with me and the girls! Helped Alyssa through rehab. We even talked marriage… which he didn't seem too keen on…

Crap. Maybe he really has abandoned me. He's sick of me bossing him around. He wants to be free of me and my weight insecurities, free of my panicky nature. But, oh, the flirty bantering. And the sex! We connect on every level, every time.

Fuckity. I don't know what to think! He left me in such a rush at Alyssa's place that day. One moment we were kissing, the next, I was standing alone with a pot of freshly planted watermelon seeds. He'd seemed so engaged, so wanting to be a part of our family, to be my soft place to fall. Maybe, in the end, he couldn't handle the chaos that was happening with our family. Or maybe he's simply trapped in another time. Either way, it breaks my heart because I know we're supposed to be together. I know it.

Ashooooooga... Ashooooooga... Ashooooooga!

Oh, for the love of... peace and quiet! Turns out that Cici snores, but only on planes where the people in the row beside you can give you Angry Owl Eyes for six hours. Excellent. All these years I've bunked with her, I've never heard Cici snore. She chose to start today. Her chest, covered in a blanket of her flowing red hair, rises up and down with her every breath. She looks almost angelic. She's so much less trouble when she's sleeping.

A Stealers Wheel tune starts playing in my mind, and no thanks to a freakish date I narrowly escaped a few years back, I can't help changing the lyrics:

Gram complaining about her butt floss to the left of me,

snorer to the right,

here I am, stuck in the middle with...

...the visibly irritated man behind me, who's taken off his running shoes, revealing a putrid case of foot B.O. that makes me wish I had a bad sinus infection.

Gene, I love you, but when I finally find you, we are never, ever flying anywhere.

Four hours later, I'm sweating bullets, pushing Gram in a wheelchair down the gangway while trying to stop my carry-on from slipping off my shoulder. Of course, no one at Charles de Gaulle airport is helping me. The attendants are far behind us, flirting with each other. Cici went ahead to the airport to find an attendant to get a wheelchair, but it turns out there was already a wheelchair on the plane. Something was lost in translation, *je crois*.

"I can do this myself, Cat," Gram grumbles. "I've got two arms. Probably could have walked it, too. You girls didn't let me try." She starts to push herself away from me, like she's trying to win a triathlon. I wonder if she packed a swim cap.

As I let go of her chair and hoist my carry-on back onto my shoulder, my gaze catches my daughter's as she walks down the gangway: a supermodel strutting down the runway, rocking a black mini-dress and boots. Unlike me, she's not frazzled, not perspiring, and has no dark circles under her eyes. I want to know what anti-frizz product she uses on her newly pageboy cut chestnut hair, and how is she not tripping over those gorgeous black stiletto boots? I would, and I'd probably end up in a viral YouTube video in the process.

That's my baby. My 20-year-old baby. The one I nearly lost. I wouldn't even say I feel relief that the Goth look is gone. If she loved and kept it until her 60s, I could have loved that look on her, because it was her.

I choke back tears and try to stay focused on the present moment, which feels like one of those slow-mo frames in a touching Oscar-nominated film. I'm so glad we've made it this far. I'm so relieved my baby's alright.

"Ouch! That was my foot!" I fall to the floor, writhing in pain, and attempt to massage the foot a man just bashed his cart into.

"Pardon, madame, excuse moi." A tall, thin young man in

a dark grey suit and dark glasses takes off his black fedora and puts his hand on my back. "It was, how you say, accidental," he says in a strong French accent. "I hope you are not hurt." He waves his passport in my face and heads off in the other direction, leaving me a crumpled mess on the ground. Super. If this is typical of Parisians, I'll be the one in the wheelchair by the time May 4th rolls around.

Wheelchair. Come to think of it, I don't remember hearing Gram bawl out Mustache Man. That's so out of character for her.

"Mom!" Alyssa rushes up to me, but turns her head back at the young man, now a tiny black speck in the distance.

"You Asshooooole!" she calls after him. Never one to mince words, my girl. I notice an older woman in a black turtleneck and bright red lipstick staring at her, and Alyssa points to the Canadian Flag on her backpack and flashes the woman a grin. The woman's expression immediately switches to a jovial one. She actually looks like she's contemplating giving Alyssa a hug.

Cici's by my side, helping me up.

"Cat! You okay? Sorry, I couldn't find a wheelchair, and then I couldn't find you, and then I couldn't pass up free samples at Starbucks." She gives me a sheepish smile and holds up an iced coffee with whipped cream on top. "Let's get Gram, grab our luggage, and get out of here. She in the restroom?"

I stand up, brush some dirt off my jeans, and glance around. Where'd Gram go?

"Uh, yeah, that's probably where she is." I head over to the ladies' and call in. "Gram! We're out here waiting, okay?"

We wait, and wait, and wait. Ten minutes pass. Fifteen. My heart is beating fast. I return to the restroom and do a thorough once-over, opening every unlocked cubicle, accidentally exposing a horrified, middle-aged brunette reading OK! Magazine on the toilet as I do so. “My bad! So sorry!”

I rush out, kicking off that string of sticky toilet paper that’s been attracted to my left shoe since 1982. It looks like I’m doing a pathetic attempt at the latest dance craze, plus, I’m in a mild panic, so I’m getting a lot of staring from passersby.

By the time I return to Cici and Lyssa, they’ve put our carry-ons on a cart and are racing up and down the wide hallway, calling, “Gram! Grammie!” Cici’s closest to me, so I put my hands on her shoulders to stop her and grab her gaze.

“Cici. You’re wasting your breath. I think she’s really gone.” I point to the empty wheelchair beside the escalator. It looks like the exact one Gram was using.

“She’s gone? She’s gone! Holy crap, Cat, we should be jailed. We’ve just lost our ninety-four-year-old grandmother in one of the busiest airports in the world.”

My knees start to buckle. No. I will not faint. Not this time! I find the nearest bench and sit down. I want to pump my fist in the air, curse the heavens. And pee. I never did get a chance to pee.

All we’ve been through these past few months... all we’ve been through as a family... and now this?

Chapter Seventeen

Charles de Gaulle Airport

Sunday, April 30, 2017

10 a.m.

Cici looks up at the security guard, a man so intimidating and muscular he deserves a cape with a giant S on it, and bats her eyelashes in a pathetic attempt at seduction.

"Sir, we think our passports have been stolen, and our grandmother is missing! We need your help!"

"Come with me." We get up off the bench, I grab our carry-on luggage cart, and all three of us follow Super Securité Man.

The guard has a slight French accent and speaks sternly, but has a blank expression on his face. I can't read it. I can't figure out if he's amused by Cici, doesn't understand a word she's said, or thinks she's a major criminal. He hasn't handcuffed us yet, so I think we're alright. We follow him down a long hallway to a tiny office with the words *Securité* on the door, a small desk, and a couple of plastic chairs. He asks us to sit down and starts speaking a flurry of French words I don't understand into the walkie-talkie attached to his belt.

Gosh, that worked well. No line-ups. No forms to fill in. They'll capture the criminal who nabbed our passports and we'll quickly be on our way. I love my sister!

Three hours later

Sunday, April 30, 2017

Charles de Gaulle Security

I hate my sister.

This is all her fault. She shouldn't have approached airport security. We should have reported the passports stolen at a proper police station. These dudes actually think we're terrorists!

"You have no photo I.D. How can we let you into our country?"

While I'm having a mild panic attack about our missing grandmother and passports, Cici's simply getting angry. She takes a deep breath, but her face still looks like a ripe tomato. This is not good. You don't get angry with someone in a uniform. Not a good idea.

"But I'm trying to explain to you, you already did! We've been through customs! Since then, our passports were *stolen*. We didn't bring drivers licenses. We were just going to take the Métro and cabs everywhere."

Super S glares at her, runs his fingers through his short, dark hair, and exhales.

"C'est des conneries!" he shouts.

I have no clue what that means. What did he say? Is he going to call Sean Connery? That wouldn't be so bad. He's my favorite Bond.

He spews forth a few more French words I don't understand, so I grab my carry-on briefcase off the cart, unzip it, and start to take out my phone to read Frommers.com for a translation. Super S guy reaches over and grabs my phone, then places it on the filing cabinet where I can't touch it. Oh. My. God. Are we under arrest here? What's going on?

"I will try to explain one more time. Your passports were taken, yes? You have no proper photo I.D., therefore our police cannot file a missing person's report. You have no identity," Super S says.

"I do," Alyssa, who's been sitting silently in a wooden chair in the corner pipes in, waving the passport she'd been carrying in her purse. "I'm the smart one who carried mine in my purse. So, like, can I go now? I really want to see the Eiffel Tower."

Cheeky girl! I do like that she's got her sass back. That's a good sign, but, just not the best timing.

"Alyssa, please be quiet. This isn't helping." I don't want to get angry at her, but I don't need her dry sense of humor right now.

"Sir, can't you look up our passports? You'll see we have proper ones," I say as politely as I can.

"Yes we have your records," he says with his slight French accent. It's creeping me out. I truly feel like I'm in a spy movie, but sadly, minus Sean Connery!

Super S turns his laptop around to show us his screen. "I have you, Katherine Glamour; your record is flagged *ici*, here. There is a flag from Canadian border officials. This is why I have you here. I am not that certain your record is clean, ladies. I must look into this matter."

He turns the laptop back around, gets up from his desk, stops at the door a moment, and stares at us, then closes the door behind him. Click.

"Is that a key in the door? Is he locking us in? Plus, he has our phones! He can't do this! This is an outrage! We're not criminals! We need to get out of here and find Gram!" Cici stands up and looks about to pound the glass door with her fist when Alyssa grabs her arm and pulls her away from the door.

"Auntie C, seriously, this isn't some TV show. You aren't going to make more fans by being the hero, here."

Cici sits down beside me and exhales deeply. "I guess you're right. But what the hell is he even talking about? You're flagged, Cat? Flagged? What the hell for?"

I pause to think a minute. Then I have it. My throat immediately feels constricted with fear.

"Oh no. No, no, no! Vermont! Don't you remember?" I'm feeling dizzy and a little nauseous. "That time we crossed the border accidentally, without going through customs!"

Alyssa starts to laugh hysterically. I try to clamp my hand over her mouth, but it only muffles it a little.

"Well this is a shit mess we're in, now!" Lyssa keeps laughing. "I mean, messier than Marmie on a feeding frenzy!"

She suddenly stops making loud noises and mutters, "Oh crap. My record. Thank God I made that deal so I wouldn't have charges pressed against me.

Cici is pacing back and forth, but the room is so miniscule, she looks like a small, fragile doll pacing inside a dollhouse. "Cat! That incident – that was our GPS's fault! Blame the dumb GPS for taking us across the border that day without taking us through customs!"

"He'll call the Canadian border officials and straighten this whole thing out," I tell Cici, but even as I say it, I feel my hands shaking. I know what happened in Vermont. What happened in Vermont should have stayed in Vermont, but me and my big mouth, and guilty conscience – I had to call the Canadian Border office and confess our sin!

"Uh hello? I had an, er, problem at the Vermont border I wanted to report?" I held the phone up to my ear tighter because it seemed to be a poor connection.

"Yes ma'am, go ahead with your complaint," a woman replied in a monotone voice.

"Oh, well it's not really a customer complaint or anything," I said, staring out my window as I spoke. I looked at the beautiful garden across the street, trying to relax my nerves. "I wanted to report a... a breach of security, I suppose?"

"A breach! Ma'am what are you talking about?"

"Well, see, me and my sister and daughters went shopping in Vermont today, and when we drove back, it was really dark, like, pitch dark, and I was keeping my eyes on our GPS to make sure we found our way back to Canada, but, um, the GPS must have taken us through some back roads, because suddenly we looked up and saw a Welcome To Canada sign, and we hadn't even gone through the customs check point."

The woman was silent a minute. "Shit. Not again."

"Again? This has happened before?" I coughed, choking a little on my own saliva.

"Yes, Ma'am, unfortunately, a couple times. We're looking into putting flower pots there so cars can't go through," she muttered.

I couldn't help it, I knew the phone call was probably being recorded, but still, I burst out laughing. "Flower pots? You're planning on solving a major cross-border security problem with *flower pots?*"

"Ma'am I'm going to have to ask you to call another number. I could have you fined or even arrested for not going through customs."

"What?! You've got to be kidding me! I did the ethical thing, here! The ethical thing! I called to report the problem!" I could feel excess sweat slowly trickling down my front chest and armpits. I don't want to go to jail! I look horrible in orange.

"Nevertheless, ma'am, I could have you arrested, so, don't make fun of the flower pots."

"Uh, okay..." I had to bite my lower lip. "What number do I call?"

"I can put you through. Wait on the line."

I waited and waited for about 20 minutes, then was finally put through to someone named Lester. I wondered how long he'd been working at the border, with an old school name like Lester. Maybe Lester was in charge of Moving Flower Pots to confuse Americans trying to get into Canada illegally. Good job, Lester, good work.

I spoke to Lester, he filed a report, and told me to, "never to speak of this again."

Of course, I did speak of it again. I told Gene just the other week, a few friends at the gym, and Gram's poker pals. Come on, it's a great party story!

Maybe that's why I was Flagged.

I can't sit still, anymore. I join my sister, pacing beside her, our strides falling almost in unison. Alyssa begins rummaging through her carry-on.

"You two can stop pacing, now. I have good news."

I stop and stare at her. "Good news? You found Gene in that bag of yours? Because seriously, Lyssa, he's the only one that could pull us out of this mess."

"Not likely, I love the guy too, okay?" Her face turns soft. Vulnerable. "He stood by me when Jimmy and a lot of my friends chose not to. But, he's without magic, and MIA, Mom. You need to let it go..."

"Let it go, turn away, and slam the doooor!" Cici stops pacing and starts singing and spinning, arms wide open, face to the ceiling. Maybe she's finally lost it.

"Stop it, both of you, you aren't funny!" This is not a good time to have to try to choke back tears.

"Mom, I'm serious, I may have a solution, here." Lyssa pulls out three sheets of paper from her bag.

"I wanted to be prepared for this trip. I read on Google that it's a good idea to have a copy of your passport. So, I scanned them. I never thought we'd need these..."

I sit down, grab the papers from Lyssa, and look at all three.

They're scans of our passports. This proves we have identities! Maybe Super S will be satisfied with these.

Speaking of the devil, Super S unlocks the door, comes in, and sits at his desk without looking up. He's reading his phone.

Alyssa marches up to his desk and shakes the papers under his eyes. "Here. *Voici*. You'll want to see these."

Super S studies the papers carefully. He studies each paper, looks at each of us, then clears his throat. "*Alors*. Your border officials have texted me back. They say you are no threat to us, but they will be calling you when you return because they wish to see your..." he rereads the text, as though to assure he's gotten the rather confusing message right. "GPS machine?"

Alyssa snickers loudly. "I don't think our GPS machine is a threat to our national security, officer. I think, though, that those dufuses at the border might be..."

She puts her hand over her mouth when Cici glares at her. I'm still finding it hard to speak. Are we finally out of this mess?

"You must report your stolen passports, now," Super S says.

"What?" I've found my voice, and it's full of rage. "We've spent over three hours here with you, doing exactly that! We told you they were stolen and that our grandmother is missing when we started this whole inquiry. Didn't your report that?"

"*Oui madame*, we called the *policiers*. They have the first report. You must file a detailed report in person at this address." He hands me a slip of paper.

"A detailed report? What is this, college?"

He ignores me and continues without looking up. "After, you must go to the Canadian Embassy to replace your passports. Good day." He hands us each our phones and ushers us out of his office, where the rest of our luggage is waiting for us. I barely have the energy to tow my carry-on behind me, let alone my suitcase. I want to curl up in a ball on the nearest bench and sleep, but I have to keep going. I have to find Gram.

Cici kisses her phone, then starts scrolling it madly, taking it all in like a woman inhaling a cigarette after a long plane ride. "Oh, I missed you so much!" she says out loud to her phone as she walks. Pulling her suitcase behind her, she scrolls through her messages. I'm in awe of how she does all this so effortlessly, without bumping into anything. Alyssa rolls her eyes at Cici and walks ahead of us.

"Any texts from Gram?" I ask Cici as we follow Lyssa outside.

"None, yet. I'm sure she's gone ahead to the hotel. Maybe we panicked too early. Maybe we'd be silly to report her. You know how she likes to do things on her own."

"But wouldn't she have texted us by now?"

"Not if her phone is dead. She always forgets to charge it," Lyssa answers.

"No, I still think we should go to this address. We'll go after supper. Let's eat and check into the hotel first."

The evening air is chilly – it can't be more than 10 C. We zip up our coats and look around for a cab. There are many circling around, but all are taken.

Finally, I manage to hail one, and we pile inside. The cab stinks of cigarettes and air freshener. I just want to get into a warm bed; I feel like I've been hit by a truck.

"Okay, Cici, what's the name of the hotel Gram booked?"

"That's, um... with Gram." Cici looks down at her hands.

"You don't even know what hotel Gram booked?" I shout. "Lyssa? Any idea?"

Alyssa scrolls her phone, searching. "I didn't save it. I thought you had it, Mom."

"Fuckity!" I can't take this anymore. Some vacation.

The cabbie adjusts his rear view mirror and catches my eyes. He looks at me like I'm some Crazy Lost Canadian. Which I'd say is exactly right.

"We aren't familiar with the hotels? Can you...?" I say, hoping he knows where to take us. Surely, he'll know.

Chapter Eighteen

Sunday, April 30, 2017

8 p.m.

Honk!

"Nique ta mere!"

Noises startle me awake. First I hear the car horn, then the cabbie swearing in French. I'm pretty sure whatever he's saying about the other cabbie's mother isn't very nice. Not nice at all.

Cici and Lyssa stir, too. They rub their eyes and look around. We must have fallen asleep. Great, we missed all the Parisian sights, too.

The cab pulls up in front of an old building and screeches to a halt. It's getting dark out, but I can just make out the sign: *Hotel Familia*. It's slightly crooked; its paint is peeling. I want to weep. I suppose the cabbie is either "familiar" with this hotel, or thought that I was asking for it.

I look at the building, its false balconies blossoming with bright red flowers, and give the front entrance another once-over. It's definitely not five-star luxury, but from what I can see, it's not the *It* spot for the Annual Cockroach Convention, either.

"Okay everyone. This will have to do. Let's give it a try." I give the cabbie some Euros I got at the bank back home. At least we have some cash and credit cards. All is not lost: just our passports, and our elderly grandmother.

"Merci," I tell the cabbie as he loads our bags onto a luggage cart near the hotel's front doors.

The woman at the front desk is amicable enough, but I'm not so sure what to expect from a two star hotel in France. The elevator must be over 100 years old, and the ride up is so rickety I have to hold onto Cici's shoulder for support.

I'm worried sick about Gram. Sure, she likes her independence, but we're nearing 24 hours without hearing a word from her. What if she's ill? What then?

Alyssa's the first one to hit room 411 when we reach the fourth floor. She puts the old key in the lock, turns it, and has to give the door a little shove with her hip before it opens.

We all walk in, slide off our shoes, and drop our carry-ons in the hallway. The room is bright and painted some odd hue of orange. The walls are adorned with large paintings of scenes from Paris, and the curtains are covered in a pattern of tiny black

Eiffel towers. It's cute, and it looks clean, but it's tiny. The king bed is covered in a ruby red duvet with gold trim. It could be almost regal, if three of us weren't sharing it. Lyssa flops down on the bed, covering most of it with her outstretched body.

"We're sharing the bed? One bed?" She groans. "Even a king bed doesn't give me enough space to avoid your prickly legs!"

"Oh, thanks, Lyssa, and you're a vision of beauty in the morning, you and your eye-cover that has fake eyes on it. Creepy." Cici complains.

"Don't get me started on your snoring," I say to Cici and throw myself on the bed beside Lyssa, pushing her aside a little. "This is the only room they had left. It's April in Paris. It's a popular time for tourists."

"Almost May, isn't it? Tomorrow's the first, Mom," Lyssa corrects me.

"I don't know what day or time it is, and I don't care. All I know is I need to sleep," Cici says and falls over dramatically into the empty spot beside me. I shake her, but she won't budge.

"Cici, get up, we should call the police. See if they've found Gram. See if we have to go in to the station."

"Mffffph," Cici mumbles into her pillow. I'm afraid we've lost her for the night.

Lyssa rubs my back a little, consoling me like I did her in hospital. It feels comforting and reminds me of how far we've come these last few months. There was a time I thought she'd never stop throwing books at me.

"Gram will text soon, Mom. She's off doing her own thing. Remember gambling? You told me all about it. You thought she was trying to tell us something: that she wants more space and her own adventures. You need to let go." She coughs, and turns her body away from me. She's probably afraid I'm going to lose my temper.

Instead, I lose my will to stay awake. I decide to let go of control – as if I ever had any control – over this so-called vacation. I pull up the covers and push my face deeper into the fluffy pillow.

As I close my eyes and drift off into la-la land, I see Gene, greeting me at our castle.

Chapter Nineteen

Monday, May 1, 2017

9 a.m.

We're sitting on the cold, blue marble floor, our backs against the wide wooden doors of the Canadian Consulate office. We've been waiting here for an hour. We, meaning, me and Cici. Lyssa was dead to the world when I tried to wake her. I left her a note, asking her to please not leave the room until we returned.

I trust her more than ever after our successful family counseling sessions, but I'm not stupid. You don't leave a recovering addict alone to roam the streets of Paris. Well, maybe you do if you want to film a cool reality show. Not me.

I check my phone, hoping for a text from Gram, or the police, then look up at the clock on the wall. I wanted to get to the police station sooner than this. I can't believe this office is still not open at 9:05 a.m. What's going on? Maybe we should head to the station, then come back here.

Cici looks at the clock, looks at me, then gets up and walks around a little. After she paces the hall a couple times, she leans back against the wall and notices a door to another room that's being held open by a door-stopper. Behind the door is a gold-framed sign on a metal stand with its front facing the wall. She gives me an inquisitive look, then shrugs her shoulders and starts to pull the sign out from behind the door.

"What are you doing? That was put away for a reason!" I try to whisper, but my voice echoes down the hall.

"Oh you think so? You don't think it's of value to us?" Cici points to the message. It reads:

> ***Please note that Honorary Consuls are not employees of the Government of Canada. As a consequence, they have other professional obligations and commitments. Occasionally, they may be absent from their offices. We suggest you call before going to the Consulate.
> ***

Well that's great. We didn't call first, we're here, we're tired, our asses are freezing cold, and the Honorary Consuls are absent?

So. Even in one of the most romantic cities in the world, Mondays suck.

"*Oui Mesdames?* Can I help you?" A tall, thin gentleman with white hair and black-rimmed glasses pops his head out from the door of the other room.

"Oh, is this where we can be issued emergency Canadian passports? Ours have been stolen." I get up off the floor and brush off my pants. Maybe this is it. Maybe now we're getting somewhere.

"No, no, that office is closed for today," the man says, but he looks genuinely concerned for us.

"Can't anyone here issue us some emergency passports?" Cici uses her most authoritative voice and puts her hands on her hips. "We'll need them for I.D., and to fly home in a few days," she explains.

The man rubs the stubble on his chin and looks at both of us, carefully, from head to toe as though he's a judge deciding our fates in a dance competition. Will we be thrown out of the competition for looking like disheveled travelers, or will it be 10s across the board?

"I can take down your information and have one of the Consuls contact you tomorrow. You could have the passports by..." He looks at his phone, checking its calendar. "Friday. The fifth."

"Friday!" I gasp, wanting to scream. "We're scheduled to leave Thursday."

"Well, you'll simply have to take in the sights. Stay a while," he grins wide, baring every single shiny veneer, as though deciding to stay in Paris is a no-brainer, "discover our magic."

"Listen, Mister. I know a few things about magic, and so far, this trip has been far from magical." I start to bawl the guy out. "We've lost our passports. What's worst, we've lost our grandmother! And I thought this was going to be my wedding week. My wedding week! Happy, happy, happy fucking times!

Do you even understand?" The tears start to seep out of me, from deep inside my soul, like a sudden summer downpour.

I can hear my angry voice echoing down the hall. I can feel the rage rising and heating my chest. I'm sure my face is turning bright red. Cici grabs me by the arm and pulls me away from the man. Gently, she pushes me on the shoulders and sits me down in our spot on the floor, again.

"Sit. Calm down. Whatever you do, don't get us arrested."

"Arrested! We weren't arrested! You tried to seduce a security guard!" I yell.

"Seduce a security guard seduce a security guard!" Again with the echoes. I have to stop shouting. She's right. I do need to calm down. I take a deep breath and bury my head in my hands. As I do, someone walks past me and dumps a stack of newspapers beside me, outside the closed office doors. Mmm. I do love that strong scent of freshly-printed papers, despite that newsprint often makes me sneeze. I wonder if they're French or English.

I glance at them, grab one from the pile, start to unfold it, and notice Cici talking to our helpful older gentleman. Poor guy. He sure didn't see me coming. He'll probably stop buying shares in anything Canadian after this. I've probably fucked up all hopes for our maple syrup industry in France.

Cici's taking out her phone and copying down something the man is telling her. He's also inputting information into his phone. Huh. My networked big sis; it's just like her to use her poise and charm. She's getting something done. Maybe there's hope for this holiday, yet.

"Ahh... ahhh... ahhh... *choo!*" Ick. That could be the biggest noise I've ever made.

"Choo choo choo choo!" echoes down the hall. Cici and the man look over at me. Passersby stare.

"Oh. My. *God!*" I gasp out loud, re-reading the English headline in the Entertainment section. I stand corrected. *That* was definitely the loudest sound I've ever made.

My voice echoes so loudly, Cici rushes over to see what's going on. She bends down to read the paper I hold out for her:

BAD ASS GRAM HAS A BAD ASS LOVER!

Beneath the bold headline is our beloved Gram, holding up a full cocktail glass. She's clinking glasses with a man I've never seen before, who looks to be in his 70's. On his left arm there's a dragon tattoo, his right nipple sports a ring, and on his chest is a patch of curly white hair. Naked from the waist up, he's, sitting in a hot tub, his arm around Gram. They're both beaming.

Cici can tell I can't speak right now. She takes the paper from me and reads the photo-caption out loud:

"Kate Morgan, also known as Bad Ass Grandma, is vacationing at the Romantic Park-Hyatt Hotel in Paris with her French lover."

"Ew, Cici, did you have to read that out loud?" I get up and whack her on her arm with the folded paper. "I've read it about eight times, now. I know what it says."

"So, she's doing just fine." Cici sighs and places the paper back in my lap.

"Yup. She sure is. I'm heading over there to give her hell. You joining me?"

"The woman's in a luxury hotel. We're in a broom closet! What do you think?" Cici grabs her purse off the floor and waves a goodbye to the man, who nods his approval. I'm not sure what they've discussed, but Cici seems to have this covered. What's going on with Gram is of greater concern, anyway.

As we walk out of the building, I open the paper one more time and stare at the photo. It's right there in gruesome full color, but it's still hard to believe.

Gram has ditched us for an old dude with a nipple ring.

Chapter Twenty

When the cab pulls in front of the Park-Hyatt Hotel, a couple of young men in navy blue, gold-trimmed uniforms rush to open my door and take the luggage from the trunk. It's as if they think I'm a celebrity. I wonder if they are aware that I'm Kate Morgan's granddaughter, or is this just five-star service?

I take the young man's hand, avoid the puddle below my right foot, and step out of the cab.

"*Bonjour, Madame. Bienvenue.* Welcome to the Park-Hyatt," he says. The building that stands before me is a breathtaking work of architecture. I feel like we're in a 1940's film, and I'm the starlet.

To my left and right stand a couple of old streetlamps. Their warm glow highlights the cutout design at my feet, which is a reflection of the beautiful circular design above the main door. The main door is sliding glass, and I step up to it and float inside as if I'm Cinderella going the ball. I'm mesmerized. Momentarily, I forget about Cici and Lyssa, who loaded up the cab at the Familia while I sat fuming, newspaper on lap, in the car. I realize they're helping the Hyatt porter organize our luggage and paying the cabbie. I guess I owe them one.

As I enter the lobby, I'm overwhelmed by its Zen simplicity and elegance. There are small, black granite coffee tables placed around the edges of the room, each decorated with Granny Smith apples in oblong wicker baskets. The walls are made of bamboo. I walk closer to touch them and notice a young girl, maybe 19 or 20, standing behind the marble front desk, smiling at me.

"Hello," I say, and hear my voice echo. "I'm actually looking for a guest here... Kate Morgan?"

"Ah yes, isn't she lovely?" The girl beams. "I'm sorry, but for her safety, I must ask for your I.D."

Shit. My ID. Here we go. "You may not believe this, but our passports were stolen. We're waiting on replacements. Will this do?" I take out my Visa Gold and the scan of my passport and hope for the best.

"Ms. Glamour. You're her granddaughter, aren't you?" The girl's voice becomes more high-pitched.

"Yes." I blush, not realizing I had any notoriety in Canada and the US, let alone France.

"I've seen the PSA's that you did with her. I'm actually from BC," the girl says, and I hear myself exhale loudly. It's amazing how happy I am to be Canadian in this moment.

"She's in our Ambassador Suite," the girl says, "but I just saw her walking to our indoor pool and spa a few moments ago. I'll have someone show you the way."

"There are three of us. We have a room reserved here, too, under her name, but if it's okay, I'd actually like to set down our luggage behind the desk for a moment and go see her right away."

"Sure, whatever you like," she says. "It's so great to meet you!"

As I reach out to take the hand she's offering me, Alyssa comes bouncing up behind me, with Cici not far behind.

"Mom, some of the rooms have two fireplaces! I heard another guest going on about it! Two!" Lyssa is bursting with excitement. I'm pleased she's having a good time, but I'm still seething with anger over Gram's behavior. I'm trying to figure out exactly what I'm going to say to her.

"You can follow Jacqueline to the pool and spa, ladies, then we'll get you settled into your room," the girl explains as another, slightly older girl approaches us and starts leading us out of the grand lobby, to the right, and down a wide hall.

When we reach a large, glassed-in pool area, the woman takes a key card from her pocket and swipes it beside the entrance. The enormous pair of glass doors slide open, and we all walk in. I scan the area, looking for Gram. It doesn't take long to find her.

Gram is soaking in the corner hot tub beside a good looking, silver-haired man who looks to be in his late 70's. She raises a drink garnished with a pineapple slice.

"Well it's about time! It's about time, girls!" She chuckles.

As if. As if our tardiness were our fault! We wasted hours looking for her! I need to take a deep breath. This could get ugly, and I don't want it to.

"Gram, is that a Pina Colada?" Lyssa drops her jaw, along with her oversized purse, on the floor.

"Sure is. Super yummy, too. The pineapple juice is freshly squeezed! Why don't you get on your suit and join us, Princess?"

That's it. That's enough. I walk straight up to the hot tub and glare at Gram. "You had us worried sick! You disappeared on us, without a text!"

Gram shrugs and takes another sip of her Pina Colada. "So, I forgot."

"Forgot? For twenty-four hours? Gram. Is this some type of punishment? I don't think I deserve this." My heart's beating fast, but I'm holding back the tears. It's not often Gram and I argue. I hate conflict. I had enough of that with Jimmy. I just want her to apologize and be done with this.

She gets out of the hot tub and slowly wraps a large white towel around herself. Then, she shuffles up to me, looks right at me – right into me – with her wise, blue-grey eyes. She looks sorry. Sincerely sorry, but also, what's that other expression on her face? There, in her left eye. A glimmer. A glimmer of... joy. Hope. Adventure.

"Cat," she lowers her voice. I assume it's so that the man in the hot tub can't hear her. "I just forgot. I did leave the airport before you, because I wanted to show you I could get here myself. Then, I was having so much fun with Edouard, I lost track of time."

"Edouard? You ditched us. I can't believe you ditched us!"

"It's Eddie for short. And I'm sorry. I didn't mean to ditch you gals that long. I took my own cab to the hotel because I was angry about the wheelchair. I may be slow, but I'm capable of walking."

Eddie wraps a big white towel around his tiny Speedo and walks up to us, giving Gram a little pat on her behind before reaching out to offer me his hand. "Damn straight she's capable. You should see her on the back of my bike."

"*Bike?* You rode this man's motorbike? Are you sure that's a good idea?" I don't shake Eddie's hand. He drops his hand beside his hip, then awkwardly crosses his arms.

"Cat. Stop babying me! Besides, it isn't just any bike. It's a Harley."

"Oh, a Harley, well then that's fine with me, Gram, just peachy," I say in a sarcastic tone.

Gram sits on the edge of the hot tub beside her friend, Eddie. "I'm real sorry I did this, okay? I know it was wrong. I just wanted to show you I'm not ready for a home, yet. I can still do things on my own. Please. Please don't put me in a home!" She covers up half her face with her left hand. Are those tears? She's crying. I don't see that from Gram, often.

Maybe this little adventure of hers was like mine with Gene. Maybe it was necessary. Maybe I need to listen.

"Oh, Gram." I reach over and pull her into my chest, then give her a soft kiss on the top of the head. "Is that what you thought? That we're putting you in a retirement home? Where'd you get that idea?"

"Well, let's see... I'm old. Yup. That's about it. I'm old, and the people who canceled my show told me I belonged in a home..."

"That's their opinion! That's not our opinion," Cici interjects. "Those people cancel perfectly good television. They have their heads up their own assholes."

Lyssa laughs out loud. It's music to my ears, hearing her laughter echoing across the pool water.

"Cici, you're the main culprit." Gram raises her voice a little. "You took me to that pathetic excuse for an old people's home back at Christmas."

I glare at Cici. I can't believe she did that without consulting with me first. "What? You visited a home?"

"We were driving by, Cat." Cici looks at me with an embarrassed frown. "I told her we should just take a peek at it, since we were so close. I've been concerned for her health."

"Oh shut the door!" Gram stands up. "I'm healthier than the two of you put together. You, with your smoking, Cici! Do you forget you only quit a couple years ago? And you, Cat – have you forgotten about that heart attack? I'm not going to any home. I'll mess with them again if you put me in there."

"Gram, we aren't putting you in a home, not now, not until you're ready, okay?" Cici says, then adds, "Uh... what do you mean... mess with them... again?"

A wide smile spreads across Gram's once-sullen face. "When we did that tour on Boxing Day? I was bored stiff. Bunch o' old biddies were in the party room, sitting by the fire knitting. Knitting! It was five o'clock. We walked around, and I noticed that there was a bartender and a stereo in that room, but both looked dustier than the backside of a fridge. So, I got the party started... that's all."

"Got the party started?" I ask.

"I spiked the punch bowl with a flask from my purse," Gram answers.

"Gram!" Cici and I share a good long snort-laugh, both of us forgetting we're supposed to be mad at her.

"Yup. I did the deed when no one was looking, but I'm sure they'd thank me if they knew." Gram sits back down in a lounge chair. "Owners took us to look over the rooms next, and when we came back past the party room ten minutes later, those old biddies were kicking it up on the dance floor, doing the Macarena with the bartender!"

I imagine a dozen silver-haired women lined up on a

dance floor, hands on rotating hips, whooping it up like they're teenagers, and I break into a grin. I've got to hand it to Gram, the woman knows how to live. I should follow her lead and be more fearless.

"Ah ha ha!" Eddie chuckles loudly. "She sure can take care of herself, can't she? So you see, ladies, this was all just a colossal misunderstanding!" He slaps his hands on his thighs, and beams at all three of us.

Not so soon. This man is sleeping with my Gram. He's not getting out of here without the third degree.

"Edouard? Or is it Eddie? Do you have a job?" I snap.

"What the hell kind of question is that? It's Edouard Fortescue the Third, Eddie, to friends, but I'm not feeling the friendship vibe..." Eddie gets up, bends down, and starts to put on his flip flops. "Let's go, Kate. This is ridiculous. We're way-grown adults. They're treating us like children."

Gram stands up and glares at me. "He's right, Cat. Maybe I was wrong to disappear on you girls, and I'm sorry, but you forget I've been on this planet fifty more years than you. I was heartbroken when they took my show away, but Eddie here, he's been healing that hurt. He's a wonderful man, and yes, he has a damn job."

I look down at my feet. It's hard to look her in the eyes when she's ranting.

"He's a brilliant lawyer – an *avocat*, as they call it, here. He's not after my money, and he's not in some biker gang. If you gave him a chance you'd find that out for yourself. We're having dinner in our Ambassador Suite, tonight. They're doing it up all nice for us at eight p.m. You're invited, that is, if you can be nice." She slips on her purple water shoes, ties up her robe a little tighter, takes Eddie's hand, and walks away from us, straight out the sliding glass doors.

If I weren't feeling terrible for not knowing Gram thought we were going to put her in a home, I'd be blissfully soaking in all this luxury. Instead, I'm in our stunning, roomy, gold-and-blue themed Diplomatic suite, staring out a large window overlooking the park, trying to decide if I like Eddie or not. It's not like I have a bad gut feeling about him. He actually seems like he could be the perfect fit to compliment Gram's fire. But this is all happening so fast.

I rub my hands along the gold silk curtains, then turn around, catching a glimpse of myself in the opaque smoked-glass mirrors across the room. I look quite glamorous for someone who's had five hours sleep and no vacation on her vacation, yet. I did my best to get glammed up for dinner; after all, this is a fancy place, so it's an opportunity to feel elegant and beautiful.

I'm trying to set a good example for Lyssa. I remember our counselor telling me that self-talk in the mirror is one of the ways we can either strengthen or break a positive self-image. Tonight, I stood beside Lyssa and made her say three nice things about herself. Eventually, she did, although she giggled at the mirror a few times before finding three things to say. It's awkward complimenting your own image if you aren't a reality star or a Selfie Addict.

Now, it's my turn.

"I like my hair twisted in a high bun like this.

"I love how I feel in this dress. Slinky. Seductive.

"I'm not a size two, or six, or eight! But I'm fine with who I am. I'm fabulous."

That wasn't easy, but I did it! Lyssa beams at me and gives

me a little hip-check, then tucks a strand of hair back inside my bun. Earlier, we decided to try twisting my hair in a high bun, and to make my lips ruby red. I'm wearing my favorite long black dress and white pearls. I love the look. I feel sexy and classy, like Audrey Hepburn.

Lyssa is in a flowing, pastel pink gown and her hair's in an elaborate up-do. She says she learned how to do the hairstyle from a friend at the Center. The more we talk about the Center, the more I'm convinced it was the right thing to do, even though her addiction hadn't been a long-term one. We nipped the problem early. Maybe she'll never try drugs again; maybe she will. At least we have tools and resources at our disposal, if she slips back. Kind of like me and my weight. I have my own gym, my pride and joy, and so many supportive friends there. I can always get help from them if I slip back into bad habits.

I don't need Gene's magic, or his approval.

I just need *him*.

God, I wish he could see me tonight. My throat constricts, and I turn away from the mirrors. I can't cry. I can't. I need to be strong about this and believe it will all work out.

Chapter Twenty-one

Wednesday, May 3, 2017

"I'm throwing my phone in the Seines River. You can't stop me!" Cici stands at the river's edge with a look on her face that says she wants me to stop her.

Lyssa, Cici, and I are basking in the sun on the beautiful Pont Neuf, which translates in English to "New Bridge." I find that amusing, since this is, in fact, Paris' oldest bridge, built between 1578 and 1607. We've been strolling around the city after a rather lazy day by the heated hotel pool. We decided there had been enough drama, and that a few actual vacation days on our vacation were in order. The pina coladas and orange creamsicle drinks the staff brought us all afternoon were a nice touch. I could get used to that.

Since dinner with Eddie and Gram went well the other night (Surprisingly well, actually. I even told him about Gene, and he didn't spit out his food in alarm. He just listened. He actually believes us!), we felt we could leave the two of them to have their own small adventures back at the hotel (No, I don't want a more detailed image in my mind, not ever, thanks very much!) while we explored Paris for the first time.

"I'm really doing it, Cat. I need to quit the addiction. You can't stop me!" Cici repeats and inches her torso a little farther over the bridge's edge, dangling her phone over the river.

"Go ahead, sis. I know you can live without it. You know it now, too." I grin.

"Auntie C! Mom! Are you two nuts?" Lyssa tries to pull Cici back onto the small sidewalk, but Cici isn't budging. "That phone is the only one we have that's charged. What if... I mean..." She gets quiet. "What if Gene tries to reach you that way, Mom? He still could. It's not out of the realm of possibility."

I look at her face and a rush of love pours over me, warming my heart so much more than this joyful Parisian sun. She likes him, too. All that time in the Center, I wondered if she resented him, for helping put her in there, and for putting Jimmy in jail. Now, I know. She accepts him and misses him, too.

"He came to you in a phone once, Mom. Let's not risk it." She bites her lower lip and looks away from me, pretending to study the buildings across the river.

Cici stands down from the bridge ledge and puts her phone in the outside pocket of her purse. "You're right. We never know. But I've turned it off, and it stays off until we're home. I can do this."

"Thanks you two, but I don't think Gene is coming back this time." I swallow hard and turn to walk off the bridge and back toward our hotel.

"Never say never, Mom," Lyssa calls after me. The two of them hurry to catch up with my pace, but they can't. I've walked a whole block ahead of them. Someone has caught my eye. I quicken my pace. I can't lose him. I won't.

Earlier, I'd noticed him leaning against the bridge's stone wall, smoking a cigarette and staring at us for the entire cell phone incident, but I thought he was just a young Parisian interested in our drama. Now that I've thought about it, and remember where I've seen his skinny ass and black fedora before, I know it's no coincidence.

I start running, and so does he, but it seems he was caught by surprise, and if he crosses the street, he'll be hit by one of the many cars rushing to make the lights. I've got my best runners on, and I didn't clock almost an hour a day on the elliptical machine last month for nothing. He's going down.

"Stop running, asshole! We need to have a little talk." I catch up to him, reach out for his black suit jacket, and pull. It starts to rip a little at the pocket, but I keep pulling. He turns around to fight back, and there it is: the mustache. It looks fake in this light. He's just some skinny-assed 20-something in jeans and a grown-up's top hat, trying to throw us off track!

Wait. Maybe he's young and skinny, but hang on. Evaluate the situation, Cat, just like you were taught in those 15 martial arts classes. There's something shiny catching the sun's rays in his left hand, and a sinister look on his face. He's got a switchblade.

I step back for a second, get into fighting position, and kick his hand with my right foot. The switchblade lands on the pavement, so I kick it aside, then take him down with one hip toss.

"Hyaa!" I shout and feel a sense of accomplishment as he

begins to flip over my right hip and back, just as I'd envisioned. I always knew those classes, and my more substantial hips and booty, were going to prove themselves useful someday.

He's on the ground in seconds, flat on his back and moaning in pain. I use one foot to apply pressure at his neck and remain with my arms raised up in a fighting, defensive stance. He looks up at me, but the sun is glaring in his eyes, and he has to cup his hand over his brows like a visor. His face is pale white and growing whiter by the second.

"Mrs... um Mrs. Glamour? Look," he says.

I'm not surprised the kid knows my name. I just didn't expect formalities, especially with my foot at the ready to cut off his breathing any second.

"Listen, you little shit. I know it was you at the airport. You stole our passports, didn't you? I want them back, now, and I need to know why you stole them."

"Let me up, please," he sputters, and I push down harder on his neck.

"Passports. Hand them over," I say.

He slowly points to the small, crumpled black backpack that's lying on the pavement beside his head. As I bend to pick it up, Alyssa comes running up and grabs it for me.

"Jason. Jason? What the hell? What are you doing..." she asks.

"You know him? Ah, I get it. Jimmy. Jimmy's involved. Of course!" I groan.

Cici rushes up behind Alyssa and puts her arm around me. "You okay? We saw that go down from way back on the bridge. You were amazing!"

"I'm fine, our passports are in that bag, and this guy has some explaining to do," I say and don't let him up.

"Jimmy hired me to watch all of you, okay? He said do

whatever it takes to ruin your trip to France, so I stole your passports. Tried to grab Alyssa's, too, but I couldn't." Alyssa stares at Jason with disgust, then opens the backpack, looks inside, and takes out three passports.

"Jimmy is vicious. I know it was wrong, and I'm sorry, Lyssa, because we used to be friends, but you don't get on Jimmy's bad side... you just don't..." He twinges and covers his eyes protectively as Lyssa tosses the backpack at his head.

"I don't wanna end up in prison like him." He starts coughing, but I apply steady pressure with my foot. He looks at me with fear in his eyes.

"Ruin our trip?" I ask. "When I saw you just now, I thought he was having you chase us to... to kill us."

"Me too!" Alyssa pipes in. "I thought we were in an episode of Breaking Bad!"

"Ha ha ha! You'd think... Nope." Jason hesitates, then mutters, "He's got it in his head that he still loves you. He's convinced himself that he can win you back, and if he only gets a year in prison, he can remarry you and start over."

"Has he been smoking his own stuff?" I snicker. "He isn't trying to marry me, kid, he's trying to manipulate us and stop us from testifying against him." I move my foot off his neck, then approach him to look straight in his eyes, pushing hard on his chest with one fist. "That explains the first-class ticket for Alyssa, too. He wanted her to miss testifying."

"Okay, okay. You figured it out," he admits with a small, sheepish smirk.

"Well, I'm not the weak girl Jimmy used to know. Not anymore. He's going to prison for a long time, and now we can add theft and intimidation to his charges." I let go of him and bend down to pick up the switchblade.

Jason quickly gets up and turns to run, but a large crowd

has gathered around us, and they move in on him, along with an imposing pair of officers who have been talking to Cici. He turns in circles, trying to find a gap to escape from all the bodies, but can't. Alyssa, Cici, and I cross our arms and give him our most intense evil eyes. One of the officers begins to read him his rights, but he interrupts them with a string of angry curse words.

"He should have had you women killed. All three of you. You'll outsmart him every time!" he calls back as the officers pull him away, into a car.

"Mom, you kicked ass! I wish Gene could have seen that!" Lyssa waves back at the officer who took our statements, then joins me and Cici as we cross the street together.

"Can we change the topic?" I snap and immediately feel remorseful. She's trying to keep me positive. "Sorry sweetie. I'm just sick of Jimmy's stunts. He's messed with our lives too many times."

"They'll put him away for a long time, now, Mom. It'll be okay, really," she says.

I point to a little red-roofed café with a quaint terrace across the street and motion for us to go check it out. "It's getting late. Let's get lunch."

Once seated, we scan the menus and all order American-style food. Lyssa tells me she's been craving a burger for days, so we order three with cheese. We also order espressos and cappuccinos and chuckle over the tiny cups they're served in. I love the taste of the coffee, but miss the feeling of cradling a warm Grande Vanilla Latte in my right hand. Creature of habit,

I suppose.

I'm finishing the last few scrumptious fries on my plate when Lyssa breaks the relaxed silence. She's done eating, and after inspecting our passports for a good five minutes, she's started reading a British newspaper.

"Look at this, guys. There's a selfie brush that's going to enable us to take more selfies." She frowns. "That's it. I'm moving to another planet!"

I lean over and read the first line of the article. "That's a shame. I was hoping we'd start taking photos in groups again. Do you remember when we used to ask strangers to take our photos? It was a cool way to meet new people."

"I still do that, Mom. I've been trying to meet new friends since Rehab," she says.

"That's good, hon. Never stop searching for the people and places that let you be yourself."

"I won't stop. I don't want any of those old friends. I was a follower, then. Even the Goth thing I did? Following. But this, this is me. Bookish. Stylin'." She smiles and pats her pageboy cut. "Pensive. I feel more myself than ever before. I think I'm going to apply to school, Mom. Law school! I wanna kick ass like you, only, on the other side of the justice system."

I look at her and try not to cry. This is not the moment to be Blubbering Mess of a Mom. "Oh Lyssa, that is so great," I can't help but lean over to give her a sideways hug and light kiss on the cheek. Sometimes, I think the bravest thing is being yourself in a world that constantly tells you otherwise. I'm so proud and relieved that my daughter has figured that one out. I certainly hadn't done so at the same age.

I notice Cici's phone is on the table, but it hasn't vibrated this whole time. It must be off. Her knee isn't jostling up and down as usual, either. She's sitting back, taking in her surroundings, and looks relaxed. It's a refreshing change.

"So, Cici, why toss the phone in the Seines River? Why so drastic?" I take a sip of my espresso and start to unwrap the small dark chocolate on the side plate.

"I've been working so hard to make a living, even wishing hard, and leaving no left over time to make a life. Hanging out with you, here, in Paris – even though half the time we've been in trouble – well, Cat, it's made me realize I need to make that life myself. No one else is going to do it for me, not even a genie."

I pass her an extra chocolate. "I'm glad you've realized that. I've noticed since we've been on vacation that you're not as glued to your phone as you used to be."

"I think I was staying over-connected because I was afraid I wouldn't... matter anymore if I wasn't ever-present online. I thought I could be erased from existence if I wasn't connected. If I wasn't 'On Top of It All,' you know? I mean, hell, I've written a book that's selling pretty well, now, but I'm more likely to become famous by balancing a champagne glass on my naked butt. How do I explain that to my girls?"

Alyssa laughs so hard she chokes a little on her cappuccino. We stop talking as she coughs, to make sure she's alright. "You don't!" she says, wiping a bit of white froth off her lip. "Kim Kardashian is an enigma to me – to many of us! People become famous for the strangest reasons. You don't want to become famous, Auntie C."

"Naw, I don't. You're so right. I don't want fame." Cici shakes a sugar pack. "I just want the shoes that come with fame."

"Me too!" Lyssa grins.

Cici adds sugar to her cup and takes a sip before speaking, again. "Spending time with you two, and logging off, made me realize what I really, really want. What truly matters. It's relationships. I want to foster those, more. So, when I get home,

Simon and I are going to…"

"Ack! No! No more, please! We can only imagine! You don't have to go into detail!" I interject, covering my ears for dramatic effect.

"Speak for yourself, bed-breaker." Cici laughs.

Chapter Twenty-two

The early evening air is fresh and clean-smelling. It reminds me of laundry hanging on the line at our childhood home in Christmas. I take another whiff and relax into it. It's the perfect antidote to the stress I felt fighting Jimmy's little punk today, along with the sweet Chardonnay in my glass.

I'm surprised there isn't much smog in Paris, at least this week. I expected to smell the usual downtown odor of dust and car exhaust, but instead there's a strong bouquet of baguette, espresso, and sweet lilacs wafting through this tiny outdoor café. Cyclists whizz past us in a blur of bright colors, as do pedestrians on their way home from work. They carry briefcases and trendy designer purses, and most are deep in conversation. Only a few Parisians are on their phones. Most are strolling arm in arm at a leisurely pace, enjoying this warm spring evening.

Lyssa left our table a half-hour ago to go for a swim back at the hotel. We stayed for drinks. Cici's cell has been sitting on the table for the last two hours, and she hasn't touched it. She's people-watching and sipping her Chardonnay, looking especially peaceful. I wish I could record this moment, but I'm also going low-tech, today. I take a mental photograph.

"So." Cici smirks at me, one eyebrow rising higher than the other.

"So."

She knows I'm impressed she's gone this long without a text or a call. We don't need to talk about it.

"So, how are you feeling?"

"Let's see." I swish my Chardonnay around in the glass a little before taking another sip. "My youngest daughter suffered from a weed-Meth overdose. My genie – because doesn't everyone have one – disappeared for nearly four years, finally returned, and now he's disappeared again. We lost our passports and our grandmother in a large foreign city, but it turns out she actually ditched us, and the passports were stolen by a goon my ex-husband hired. Oh, and I was supposed to be getting married in 24 hours. But, for now, I'm sitting on a terrace in Paris with my BFF, drinking wine, and celebrating life. I feel remarkably great."

Cici sits back and beams at me.

"And you know what else?" I continue, "Maybe it's all the struggles we've endured with Lyssa, and all that we've overcome together on this trip. Maybe it's the wine, maybe it's the *je-ne-sais-quoi* of confident Parisian women brushing off on me, I don't know! But I feel stronger. I feel like I can finally stand on my own two feet."

"You have a company! You've been managing on your own just fine, Cat, plus now we know you can kick a hired goon's ass, too!" she says.

"Yes, but internally, I felt like I still needed Gene. I felt like I needed a man to be a whole person, that I needed his approval of my body to feel comfortable in my own skin." I swirl my Chardonnay around again and take a swig. "I don't feel that way, now."

"You don't want Gene?" Cici's eyes grow wide.

"Oh, no, I want him. I love him. I just realize now that I don't need to belong to him, or have him belong to me." I feel so free, finally expressing these thoughts out loud.

"Our love is strong enough that if he isn't ready to marry me, it will still withstand the test of time and even distance. Our love... just is. That's deep isn't it?" I start chuckling.

"But, I thought you wanted a big French wedding!" Cici says, looking a little irked. "I mean, I've been arranging for bouquets to arrive tomorrow! And using the hotel office to make special little labels on them, just like you described..."

"You have?"

"Yes, of course I have. It's your dream! You wouldn't shut up about it for months!" She laughs.

"The hotel is having the bouquets delivered to Gram's room early tomorrow morning. I've been typing up the labels for them, whenever you thought I was down at breakfast or at the pool. It was going to be a surprise! But if you don't want them..." She pouts and starts shifting her cutlery around.

"God. So it... it's you who makes them! Weird. Wow. That is so thoughtful of you." I take a moment to consider this revelation. Cici made the little tags for the bouquets! "I can't lie, I'd love the dream French wedding. I never had a special ceremony with Jimmy; we just eloped. I mean, I'd want it if Gene shows up. Which I'm sure he will. Possibly. I don't know if he will. He probably won't. Damnit! I'm so unsure what's going on with him!" I stop rambling on and on and try to gather my thoughts. I don't want to give her the wrong impression.

"It's complicated," I say after a moment's pause. "I'm complicated. I'm not some main character in a novel, having a big epiphany as a major crisis point that ties everything up in a tidy little bow."

"Of course you aren't!" she says. "You're wonderfully, perfectly imperfect."

"Is that what you say about some of your meals?" I giggle and take another sip of wine.

"No, only about you, *chica*."

"Well thanks. Yeah, I want the fairy-tale ending, okay? I'm not perfectly evolved, or mature, or certain of anything." I grin at my sister. "To hell with people who say fairytales don't exist. What do we truly know for sure, anyway? I'm not done growing, not done learning. I hope I keep learning until the day I die."

"What will you do if..." I can tell Cici isn't sure how to word it, but I can read her mind.

"If he doesn't come back for me?" I take a deep breath before answering. "I'm not sure, Cici. I'm not sure." I look down at my plate, then back up at my sister. "I'd carry on, I guess. I've got a good thing going with The Cat Walk, and I want to get that delayed expansion underway. I'm not sure how I can manage all the finances and marketing along with the coaching I'm doing, but I'll find a way. I've made it this far on my own." I force a smile, then whisper. "But I'd fucking miss him."

"I know honey. I know," she says softly and passes me more dark chocolate, and our liter of wine.

Chapter Twenty-three

May 3, 2017

11:30 p.m.

The sweet, intoxicating scent of lilacs fills the air. White lights hang from the majestic oak trees along our cobblestone pathway, twinkling on and off every few seconds. Everyone is unusually quiet as we stroll through the hotel gardens toward the pool area where Gram and Eddie are supposed to meet us for wine and dessert.

I'm not sure why they want to meet us so late. It seems to me that the idea only came to them this evening, when they realized how warm and inviting it was by the pool, and they spontaneously leapt on this plan.

They seem like that kind of couple, which means, we could be in for years of last-minute adventures. Life is short: I'm up for it!

Dressed in our elegant clothing, opting for flats, and casual hair styles, we make our way down to the pool area.

After spending a few hours with Eddie here and there these last few days, I have to admit, I admire the guy. Any man who can handle my Gram's fire while not putting it out is alright with me. It took a while for me to decide, but I like him. He's solid to the core.

As we turn the corner, I immediately see Gram's slender silhouette lit up by a bright pool light behind her. She's wearing a flowing, white chiffon halter-top gown, and her hair is in an up-do, decorated with tiny baby's breath. White dress? Flowers in her hair? Wait, what?

"Welcome to our wedding, kids!" Eddie walks towards us and tips his black, Victorian-style top hat. His elegant suit matches the hat, with its silk black puff tie, gold pants, and waistcoat. A bearded man in a dark suit holding a crumpled sheet of paper, which looks like it could have been printed out from a site called GetMarriedInFive.com, flashes me a wide grin. I don't even want to ask where they got this guy. Just... no.

Gram steps forward and grabs Eddie's hand. "Cat, I know the universe has hinted that it could be your wedding day at that castle tomorrow, so here's hoping you won't mind that the old folks are exchanging vows tonight. We just couldn't wait, cupcake."

"Gram, I don't care about who gets married first, not at all. I'm starting to wonder if my wedding is anything but a fantasy, anyway, since we're missing the groom." I look over at Cici, who immediately looks the other way.

"I do worry that you're making a bad choice," I continue. "Don't take this the wrong way but... you're old. Why remarry, now?"

"Yeah, don't you remember tweeting this, Gram?" Alyssa has her phone out and is scrolling Gram's Favstar account, which lists her most popular tweets. "You tweeted this... I remember! So will everyone else! Look!"

<Don't get this fascination with Vampires. You wanna hang out with pasty faced men that sleep all day? Get married. You'll see.>

Eddie is leaning over the glowing phone, too, so we're all crowded around a bluish cell phone light, laughing in the dark. Gram grabs the phone and keeps scrolling.

"I also tweeted this one. Pay attention!" She reads another tweet out loud, "I try to live each day like it's my last, which is why I rarely have clean socks. Who wants to wash socks on the last day of their life?"

"So you're saying... this is one of those Seize the Day kind of moments?" I look at my Gram. She's glowing. I realize before she even speaks that whatever she says next doesn't matter. She's happy – happier than I've seen her in months – and she's with a good man. That's all I want for her.

"When you're old," she says, "you spend most of your days waiting. Waiting for meals, baths, medicine. Waiting to croak. I want to stop waiting. I want to do what I love, now. And what – and who – I love is Eddie."

I lean in and give her a kiss on the cheek, then wrap my arms around her and pull her in for a hug. "Gram, you gave up a lot to raise me and Cici, all on your own. You never seemed to need a man when we were growing up, but maybe you also didn't have the time. Now it's your time. You have my blessing." I feel tears welling in my eyes. I pull away and start to wipe them off my cheeks, then stand back to watch everyone exchanging hugs and handshakes. Look at that, we're The Waltons again. I chuckle under my breath. It's a great feeling to have so much love around me.

Our love-fest is interrupted by loud male voices shouting at us from behind the courtyard's fenced-in bushes.

"Kate Morgan! Kate! Bad Ass Gram! Gram!" The cameras start to click and flash above the bushes. Click, click, click, flash, flash. I can't make out any faces, yet, just a long line of large cameras sticking out from above the bushes.

"Look over here! Over here!" More clicking, and a brighter flash of light.

"How do you feel about getting married? How do you feel!" The shouts are growing louder, and harsher.

It's the paps. We cover our faces, and turn away. It's no use. There's a loud whirring noise above us. Helicopters! They sent helicopters? They're trying to land on the roof! They're unrelenting!

"Gram!" I shout above the noise of the helicopters and feel a gust of air pushing up at my dress. The skirt rises and bellows a little, as does Lyssa's flowing gown. My hair is blowing all over the place. It covers my face in a mess of crazy strands, so I can hardly see where I'm going. I stumble around for a minute, trying to find everyone else. As I step toward what I think is the grass, my feet feel cool water, but it's too late. I'm in the pool.

Fuckity. I curse myself for half a second and start to panic. This dress is weighing me down! I can see the light at the top of the pool, but I can't reach it... Oh God, I can't reach it!

I'm running out of breath and sinking further down to the bottom of the pool. Is this it? Oh God, this can't be it... I have so much to do still... I don't wanna die!

Splоosh! I see the bottom of a pair of white running shoes and know who it is immediately. The speed at which he reaches me takes my breath away even more, which isn't exactly a good thing in this moment.

Gene puts one strong arm under mine and uses the other one to work his way through the water, bringing us to safety at the edge of the pool. I sputter a little as I lean over the edge, catching my breath.

I'm fine. I'm fine, and he's back with me.

"I think you forgot your bathing suit, Petal." He chuckles and wipes the wet strands of hair off my face and out of my eyes. He studies me for a moment, and when he sees that my breathing is regular again, he takes my chin in his hands and kisses me hard on the lips. I melt right into it, forgetting all about the cold air, my wet dress, and the noise coming from the helicopters above us.

"There's a front page kiss for you!" he shouts out into the darkness.

"The paps are gonna have a heyday with this one!" he whispers as he gently guides me to the ladder.

Lyssa and Cici are holding big white towels for us at the edge of the pool. Once we've both climbed up, they help dry us off as best they can, wrapping towels around our shoulders. In this moment, they are more concerned about me being cold and Gene appearing out of nowhere than they are Gram's ruined wedding, but I'm not. I glance over and see her sitting beside Eddie on a patio chair, her head in her hands. This must be a nightmare for her, and it was supposed to be one of the happiest nights of her life. The paps are still clicking away, and the helicopters aren't leaving.

"You saved me! How... how'd you find me?" I shout above the noise at Gene. He points to the hotel's back door. He's right. We can't have a decent conversation about this, here.

I take off my flat linen shoes and quickly wring them and the bottom of my dress out. Then, I put the shoes back on, take Gram's hand, and run for the cover of the hotel.

When I look back, everyone's following me. Gene rushes ahead to open the door for us, his wet running shoes making a rhythmic squish squash squish sound as he does so. The lanky, bearded dude officiating the wedding is behind me. It occurs to me that he's running rather like an ostrich in heat, but I try to keep that odd image out of my mind and rush ahead inside.

Chapter Twenty-four

May 4, 2017

12:02 a.m.

We scurry into the Ambassador Suite one by one. Once everyone, including Ostrich Minister Man, are inside, I close and chain the door.

This is ridiculous. We're prisoners of the paparazzi.

Gram's pacing back and forth. The helicopters are circling

around outside, and several paps are attempting to snap photos with their telephoto lenses. Cici and Alyssa sit down on the roomy red couch and start texting their friends. So much for Cici's Phone Fast. I guess it is quite a story we're living, but can't they wait until we have a resolution? Eddie walks over and closes the curtains, muttering under his breath. Gene glances at me with that look I know and love so well: can we please be alone, now?

I walk over to the door adjoining my Diplomatic Suite and unlock it, motioning for Gene to follow. We need to talk, but first, I need to get out of these soaking wet clothes. No one notices that we're leaving, even the minister. Everyone is either texting, or peeking out the window, probably wondering when, if ever, these paps are going to leave so that the wedding can resume.

Once we're alone inside the gorgeous gold-and-blue anointed suite, Gene locks the door, rushes over to me, and starts ripping off my wet dress. I burst into giggles and help him by raising my hands over my head and unhooking my bra at the back.

Wait. What about the proud, strong, independent woman that I've become? I should be angry at him. He's got some explaining to do! Geesh, Cat, get a grip on your freaky, 40-something hormones!

Gene's lightly biting my lower lip and the nape of my neck while taking off his white dress shirt and unzipping his pants. I groan a little, losing myself in the sensation of his lips all over my skin, but I push him away. He falls flat on his back, onto the enormous, sky-blue King sized bed.

"Gene! You always do this! You know I can't have sex with you until we've talked."

"Talk is cheap, but this suite wasn't. We should use it wisely." He chuckles, but then frowns, sits up, and reaches out his hand for me when he realizes I'm not in the mood for dumb jokes.

"C'mere." He pats the bed. "We'll talk. I guess you'll want to know where I've been all these weeks," he mutters dramatically, as though I'm asking him for the moon.

I don't take his hand. Instead, I stand at the foot of the bed, grab the nearest pillow, and whack him over the head with it. "Stop joking around! You're always leaving me!

"I'm sorry. I swear it won't happen again." He lowers his voice to a near-whisper. "I'm here for good, now, Petal. I'll stay, if you'll have me."

I sit beside him, cross-legged, and look into his eyes. "You... you aren't going back to your own time?"

"I already did. You know when you were sleeping in the hospital with Lyssa? I went back then and collected Theo. I couldn't leave you. You needed me, and frankly, Katherine, I need you, too. My life was grey without you. Colorless.

"I was given a choice: stay in my world, with Theo, and have access again to all the magic I've learned, or live here with you, and lose my skills."

"You gave up your magic for me?"

"Sweetie, I don't think that was giving up much, do you?" He chuckles.

"No." I begin to smile, again. "You were never going to be an 'A' student when it came to magic. But then... Alyssa. I thought you were maybe helping us along. She healed so quickly. You weren't a part of that?"

"I'd like to think I helped a little, yes, but I was just being a regular guy. The guy who loves you." He takes my left hand and kisses the back of it, old-school style.

I look down at my lap and try to hold back tears. I'm overwhelmed: both happy and moved, and unsure of where to go with these emotions. Gene notices I'm shivering and pulls a white throw over my shoulders, tucking it around my torso.

"But you didn't answer my question... Alyssa was in the hospital weeks ago, where have you been all this time?"

"I've been building a house in Christmas, hoping you'll want to live there with me and Theo, but I do know that's a big step for us. After Cici and I had Jimmy put away, he started having me followed by a couple of his thugs on the outside. They threatened to kill you and the girls if I ever came near you again. I couldn't imagine my world without you, so I kept my distance." Gene takes my hand and traces the lines on my palm. "I've been living there a few weeks, wishing you could be with us. "

"Oh my God, Gene! Why didn't you tell me?" I gasp. "Was one of them a young man with a black fedora?"

"No, they were grown men. Scary men with guns, Katherine. I didn't want them coming anywhere near you, or the girls, so I stayed away for a while."

I nod. Now, I understand. He was protecting me, Lyssa, and Jenna.

"I'm sorry I didn't explain anything to you. I had to go back in time to Greece first to collect Theo, and then I had some officers arrest the men for loitering and threatening your life, but it took a few weeks... wait a second. Wait." He takes a breath and looks at me. "What do you mean, young man in a fedora?" He looks perplexed.

"He's been following us. No gun, but he stole our passports."

"I figured someone had stolen them! I also knew it had to do with Jimmy, once Gram texted me about it." He pulls a cell phone out of his pocket and smiles. "See? My new phone! I've become an actual member of the twenty-first century!" He looks really proud of himself.

I grab it, examining its shiny black case. "You're texting! I almost don't believe it! Gram's been in touch with you?"

"Since you all got to the Hyatt, yes. She told me all about Eddie and how you didn't approve at first, and then she invited me to her small wedding. We're pretty close friends, now, me and your Gram. That's why I came to France early," he explains. "I had to protect you. I've been trying to find out who stole your passports..."

"It's okay, Gene." I smile broadly, crossing my arms. "I fought back with a hip flip when he followed me the other day, and I had him put away."

"Fought back? Hip flip? You, Katherine Glamour, never cease to amaze me!" He leans in and kisses me on the eyelids and eyebrows – his signature kiss. I close my eyes and melt into his warmth. I've missed this.

"I guess I don't need to take care of you, after all," he whispers in my ear.

"No, I can take care of myself. But there are definite... areas... you can take care of for me," I whisper back. Gene caresses my back, and we gently fall onto the bed, lying face to face.

"So... Theo. He's really here? When can I meet him?" I ask.

"He's on his way here, right now, with Jenna. I wanted them to be here for the wedding."

"The wedding..." I gasp.

"I never thought I'd be proposing like this, Katherine," he says. "Shirtless, and with my pants half-open. But that's us. Unpredictable and never dull. I think I should go with it, just like we always do..." He gets up, gently pulls me so I'm facing him, and gets down on one knee on the floor. Then, he takes a small, grey, velvet box out of his pocket.

"Cat! Cat! You aren't going to believe this!" My sister has unlocked our suite with her key for the front door and is standing there holding a couple of the red rose bouquets she had made. Crap. Great timing, Cici. Great timing, as always.

"Oops. I'm interrupting something major, right? Shit." Cici covers her mouth.

Gene frowns, sighs, puts the velvet box back in his pocket, and zips up his pants. "Hey, Cici. What's up?" He runs his hands through his hair.

I pull the white throw around me tighter and glare at my sister. "This had better be important, Cici."

"I think it is..." she mutters and approaches the bed. "The bouquets I ordered have arrived... and look! I've attached the K and E tags I made for them, but I've had a revelation. You told me the tag on the bouquet from the future said K and E, so I made them exactly like you said. We've always assumed it was you and Eugene getting married, today. But think about it! It applies to two other people, too..." She lets me and Gene look at the date tag more closely.

"Kate and Eddie," Gene and I say it in unison, then look at each other in astonishment.

"Kate and Eddie! So, it was never us? Oh my God! It was always them getting married, today?" I can't believe this.

Gene shakes his head and glances down at the carpet a minute, gathering his thoughts, then looks back up at me. "I don't know, Petal. Time is a strange concept. We traveled in time and saw and heard something together, and thought it meant one thing. Maybe it meant another."

I take a deep breath. I don't even know what to feel. I'm happy for Gram and Eddie, but I feel like the wind's been taken out of my sails a little. After much soul-searching this trip, I've learned I like myself, I can take care of myself, but I want to marry Gene!

"Who knows what time intended?" Gene says. "I think,

today, it's a matter of... your future is up to you. What do you want?" He looks right at me with deep love and great anticipation.

By now, Cici has been joined by Gram, Alyssa, and Jenna, who runs up to me and gives me a great big hug.

"Mom! I've missed you!"

I hug her back tightly, then look over at the door. Yup. There he is. I'm about to meet my lover's son, and I'm wearing only a white throw. Typical.

"Gene, can we hold off on the introductions until I'm dressed? Can I get some privacy here, people?" I say.

Gene nods and goes out in the hallway to talk to Theo and Cici. Lyssa and Jenna follow him. When he returns, it's just us and Gram in the room.

"Gram," I say. "We can't have a wedding in either of these suites. It's too noisy. We need to ditch these paps."

"Sure as hell agree with you on that one, cupcake," Gram says. "Where to?"

"The castle." I smile. "We can get there by dawn. I don't think we can make it for sunrise, but you'll have that beautiful early morning light rising over the castle walls."

"But... you and Gene..." She looks confused.

I glance at Gene. "He and I have some things to talk about, first, alone. It's okay, Gram. I'm so happy for you and Eddie. Take this." I hand her the bouquet. "Go hire a car to get us all to Mornas. Let's go have a wedding!"

Gram wraps her arms around me, then walks over and gives Gene a smack on his butt.

"You two are next! Me and Eddie, we're likely to croak first, so this worked out well." She chuckles.

"You lovebirds need some time? Take the Harley." she

throws Gene a set of keys. "We'll take Eddie's brand new Thunderbird. Hopefully we can lose these creeps and their cameras after an hour of fast driving, out on the open road."

"Actually, Gram, I have a better idea! I'll wear your floppy hat and dark glasses. They'll think we're you and Eddie on the Harley. They'll follow us. We'll take the lead and get them off track."

"But... Petal... we have things to say." Gene pouts and puts his right hand in his pants' pocket.

"Yeah, well, as much as I love your body, I don't want those things said when we're both half-naked."

"We've waited before, we'll just have to wait again."

Chapter Twenty-five

The parking garage is chilly, eerily quiet, and pitch-black. Gene turns on the LED flashlight on his Swiss Army knife, and we look around for parking spot #11.

There it is! That's the Harley Eddie told us about, and right beside that, a drop-dead-gorgeous, shiny red Thunderbird. I think I'm drooling a little. I'd date the thing, if that were even remotely possible.

"Don't worry, they may have the nicer ride, but you can have the ride of your life later," Gene jokes. I smack him on his upper arm, which is protected by his thick, black leather jacket, so he doesn't even flinch.

"Oh, you mean when I take the Harley out alone around Mornas?" I tease. I missed this bantering back and forth with him.

Gene's ignoring me; he's checking out the bike's attitude, and there's lots of that to go around. "This is one bulldog of a bike! Fat, balloon tires, an all-steel peanut tank... Hey, I read about this one! It's the Road Glide. Has an eighteen hundred c-c motor producing one hundred and fifteen foot-pounds of torque!"

He's lost me with the numbers, but I like its ruby red color and its high, plush seats. "So, what does all that mean?" I ask. He's still caressing the steel tank.

"It means that at eighty miles per hour, this baby could almost ride itself." He grins at me.

At least we look the part of Cool Biker Dudes to match this menacing machine. I threw on my favorite blue jeans, black t-shirt with a glittery Eiffel tower on it, and maroon leather jacket; he's in his jacket, black jeans, and a white T-shirt. Gram and Eddie leant us their black biker boots. I'm secretly hoping Gram lets me keep her calf-hugging, knee-high boots. They're so 'me.'

Earlier, I was wearing Gram's floppy straw hat and shades, and made a big production about shuffling across the lobby as she would, parading in front of the glass doors on our way to the parking garage. I think some paps took the bait, because I saw them running away from the hotel doors, toward the parking garage ramp. As soon as we were in the garage, I tossed the hat and shades in a garbage bin. Gram will have to find herself a new disguise; we're packing light for this adventure!

Gene grabs the black helmet that's hanging on the bike, hands me the ruby red one, and we strap them on. He climbs on the bike, then stares at me for a moment.

"You look so hot," he says. "Jump on. We have some paps to lose!"

I stand there beaming up at him. "You wanna scoot over? I'd like to give her a try, first."

His jaw drops, and he takes off his helmet, as if he's overheating inside of it. I can't help chuckling. "Petal?" He stares hard into my eyes. "You can drive a Harley?"

"Sure can. Maybe I don't know as much as you do about motors and torque, but Gram taught me how to drive a Harley when I was a teenager. I think I can handle myself, here."

I gently push him to the back seat, give his face – its expression still aghast – a quick, hard kiss, and hop onto the driver's seat. "You just sit back, and keep looking sexy!"

Gene shakes his head. "I should stop being surprised by you, Cat Glamour. I should be used to this by now." He slips on his helmet and wraps his arms tightly around my waist.

Mmm, that feels nice. "Hold on, Sweet Prince, you're in for a ride to remember!" I shout above the revving engine. After clicking the garage door opener on the key, I start to drive up the ramp and quickly pull out of the garage.

Paparazzi are everywhere. Some start chasing the bike, while others are hopping into cars. Damn. I'll have to pick up speed.

I turn the corner, but take it easy. It wouldn't be a good idea to throw this bike into a corner, so I roll with it. You can't rush it on a Harley. I know I'll be able to lose these guys in time.

I look back over my shoulder and see them all waiting at the lights behind me. Phew. Except, there's another corner and a couple of pedestrians crossing it! I'm going to have to take it wide and go around them; there's no stopping at this point.

I feel Gene squeeze my waist and shout back at him, "Don't worry, but hang on!" I trail brake and roll through the corner, taking it real wide. C'mon Cat, you know how to do this.

Okay, no one was hit, but the paps are catching up! Think quick. What will get me good pull on this bike? Alright, I'll rev it up as high as she goes and pass these three cars ahead of me as I accelerate.

I bend forward into the ride and start to smell that sweet scent of burning licorice. Ahhh! It's residual oil in the air intake, and it's all good. It takes me back to my teen years, driving Gram's beautiful, albeit somewhat less powerful, Harley. I know it's weird to love that licorice smell coming out of the air vent, but I don't think of it as oil. I think of it as character. It feels like a sign: we're going to be fine.

Once I get around this construction on the A6, according to the GPS, it should be all wide open roads from here on out. At least there are no workers out, since it's still so early in the morning. I glance back at Gene and realize he's texting with one thumb, while holding onto me for dear life with the other arm. He must be telling Gram where we are at, texting the word "Go," to let her know we've lost the paps. They'll take a shorter route we mapped out, using A6 and A7, which should confuse the paps, make up some time for them in the Thunderbird, and get them to Mornas about a half hour after us.

I exit to A7 and feel my whole body relax into the bike. It's all wide open roads, lit here and there by the street lamps that dot the highway, and the light of the full moon. It's time to enjoy the open highway. I ride the wave of torque and short shift the bike to accelerate quickly.

Oh, this feels like coming home.

Chapter Twenty-six

7:20 a.m.

May 4, 2017

Mornas, France

There it is! The Mornas Castle. We've made it in record time. As the Harley speeds up the hill, the castle walls sparkle in the pink-hued early morning light.

Gene tugs with persistence at the back of my leather jacket. Except for a speedy rest stop two hours ago, we haven't taken any time to stretch our legs. I know it's been a long ride for him, and he's told me that he wants to grab some time with me alone, before Gram and Eddie's wedding.

I look over my shoulder. No sign of the red Thunderbird, but according to Gram's text, they're right behind us. I pull into the parking lot, turn off the bike, and hop off.

"Look, doesn't that bring back exciting memories?" Gene gets off the bike and points at the castle doors. That's the 50-foot wall we had to climb over to escape when the staff at the castle accidentally locked us in. I start to giggle.

"And over there, look, that brings back sexy memories..." I point to the far tower as I take his hand, and we walk up a steep, winding path to the majestic, wooden castle doors. They're locked, but we expected that.

"I wish we could make love in that tower, again," Gene whispers and squeezes my hand. "That was one of the best moments of my life."

"Me too, sexy, but you got that text from Gram. They'll be here any minute, and so will the staff. It opens at eight a.m." I moan, disappointed in the Universe's timing.

"You never did learn anything from time traveling with me, did you Petal?" He smirks. "Time is relative! C'mere. Let's see where this path leads." He tugs at my hand and takes me off the main path, onto a winding one. It's rocky and uneven, obviously made by other adventurous souls like us. I notice that I don't feel winded by the climb at all, unlike years ago when I was carrying extra weight. My heart soars as I realize how far I've come with my goals. So what if I'm not rake-thin, or look anything like those photo shopped magazine models? I can climb a hill in France with my lover. I think that's good enough. Take that, Ledussa.

We arrive at the top of the grassy hill and the path ends. Gene takes a look around, and I put my arm around his back and follow his gaze. There's the castle tower to our left, about 40 feet away, and to our right, if we look down over the cliff at the edge of our feet, we can see Highway 7. Straight ahead, behind that highway, lay miles and miles of pristine green vineyards. It's stunning to watch the early morning sunlight glistening on the grapes. Gene pulls me in closer to his waist, and we stand together in silence, soaking in the vista.

After a few moments, Gene takes off his leather jacket and shakes it out, then places it on a patch of wild lavender on the ground and starts to bend down. "Sit with me?" he asks, and I take off my jacket and join him.

The sun has risen, and continues to rise up slowly in the pink and purple-hued morning sky. The sunrise colors are as striking as the ones we watched years ago at the castle as the sun went down. "We've had some misadventures, here, but at least we've been lucky enough to watch both a sunset and part of a sunrise," Gene says, taking my left hand, and I nod. I'm feeling nervous.

"Alright, you're not in a towel, and I think we have a few minutes before your sister comes racing up that hill to interrupt me," he says, then takes the grey velvet box from out of his jacket pocket. Suddenly, the expression on his face grows serious.

"Katherine, I didn't plan our wedding day here for you, because I hadn't even proposed, yet. I felt that you deserved a proper proposal, first." He opens the box and reveals a glistening diamond ring. I'm no good at knowing one ring setting from another – never was that much of a girly-girl – but I do know this is called a solitaire. It's stunning. I've stopped breathing.

"I know I told you I wanted to date you, first, like normal people do, but I thought about it, and since when were we ever normal?" he says.

I finally breathe in again, and start to chuckle. As I do, I smell wild lavender wafting in the warm breeze around us. It's intoxicating.

Gene doesn't get down on one knee; he's already sitting right in front of me. We're on even ground – our eyes parallel with each other. It's how it should be. We're partners. He takes my left hand in both of his, and I notice his eyes are glistening with tears. "I would be so proud to be your husband, Cat Glamour. Would you marry me... tomorrow?"

"Tomorrow!" I jump up and gasp. "Get out of town!" I laugh.

"Well, we can't really have people saying, "May the fourth be with you," every anniversary, can we?" he says, and stands up, too.

"I wanted to surprise you, and you're not easy to surprise, Katherine."

I smile and cover my face with one hand. I can't believe this. He has surprised me!

"Yes. Yes, a thousand times, yes!" I squeal. Oh, here comes the ugly cry. My whole face is scrunching up like a small prune. I can't help it. He puts the ring on my finger, and I lean in for a long, passionate kiss. I'm not sure whose tears I'm feeling on my cheeks, mine, or his. We're both crying and laughing, and looking down at the shiny new ring on my finger.

"Gene." I take a deep breath. "It didn't matter what your last name was before, but now we'll have a certificate, and I'll be introducing you to people, and I don't think 'my genie' is going to cut it."

"I'll tell you my full name, but please don't take it. Keep your own. Yours is glamorous. Mine's just great." He wipes a tear off my cheek.

"Great? Ha, I can get this! Magnifico? No, that'd be Italian."

"I am Eugenius Megalo, and yes, it means great in Greek," he says and does a fancy royal bow before me.

"Alright, alright, watch the ego. Most of the time you're pretty great, but, you don't have your magic, anymore. How did you plan a surprise wedding in France for me without it?"

"Sure, I've lost my magic, but I've discovered something much stronger than magic." He grins and pulls out a gold Visa card from the wallet in his jeans.

"Credit."

"Now, now, I hope you aren't starting nasty habits so early on in our marriage." I chuckle.

"Don't worry, Gram offered to help out until I get my first paycheck."

"Paycheck? You found work?"

"I'm doing some roofing, for now. People hired me when they saw... our... can I say our? House. I'm also wondering if you need help at the gym..."

He looks down at his feet. I know asking me for help isn't easy for him.

"Yes, this is so exciting! Of course you can call it ours, but I get to pick the counters and cupboards and stuff, if it's not too late?"

He gives me a nod.

"*Mi casa es tu casa*," he says, and I love that I get what he means.

"And of course I can use your help at the gym. I hate asking for help, but it's time I admit that I can't do everything on my own."

We sit back down on our jackets, and I notice my hand is shaking a little. He notices it, too, so he takes it and slides it under his armpit, giving it a squeeze. I beam up at him.

"So, am I going to like my own wedding?" I ask, realizing I already sound high-maintenance. Well, come on! A woman has to like her own wedding day, even if the groom's been romantic enough to plan it. Besides, I wouldn't say I'm high-maintenance. I'm unpredictable maintenance. He should probably call his insurance company for an estimate.

"You don't think I've been consulting for days with Gram, Cici, and your girls? I'm pretty sure we have all the flowers, colors, and food you want, and if not, well, we'll do it again in Christmas, with all your coworkers. Uh... maybe just spend a little less, okay?"

I look down at my lap and take a deep breath. This is amazing. For years, I imagined our wedding day would take place here, at the Castle, and then when life got messy, I began focusing simply on the here and now. I stopped imagining, stopped waiting. I didn't want to live all my days waiting for my life to begin. This moment has proven to me that the best things in life happen when you aren't waiting for the best things in life to happen.

"So, where are we going?" I look up at his piercing green eyes.

"You wanted a French wedding, and you'll have it: In the gardens at Baumanière, a fancy hotel in Provence. Gram helped me find and book it. She has a bit of pull, thanks to her fame, so they are more than willing to accommodate us. We can leave after her wedding and get there by tomorrow. It'll be Gram and Eddie's honeymoon, and our wedding. What do you think?"

"I think it's perfect. But wait a second," I continue, "I thought I sent Gram and Eddie here to the castle, to be married. I thought that was my idea."

"That's what we wanted you to think, but, no." He smirks. "We just wanted to throw you off. I was never going to propose half-naked in a hotel room! I wanted to surprise you and propose here. I texted Gram the idea, and she and Cici did the rest. They even tipped off the paparazzi, to make it impossible for Gram and Eddie to get married at the hotel."

"You people! You're always up to no good!" I give him a little shove with my shoulder. "And you know what? I absolutely love it."

I start replaying all the events of the last week in my mind. "Uh, wait, though. The stolen passports? That hired kid who followed us?"

"Oh, that was all real. You really kicked his ass! There's no way we could have planned that any better than it turned out, and we definitely couldn't have hip-flipped him any better than you did," Gene says.

"I guess this proves that even time travelers can't predict the future, huh? I don't think either of us saw this moment coming, or the wedding date changing."

"Nope, you can't predict anything. For example," I lower my voice to a whisper, "do you know what I want to do with you next?" I start kissing him, unzipping his jeans, and untucking his t-shirt.

"Katherine," Gene laughs, "really, you know I'd love to, but your family's having a wedding in, oh, twenty minutes?"

"Perfect. We can squeeze in a quickie." I start licking his nipples and moving my tongue down the middle line of his chest, lower, lower, lower.

"Oh, God." He lies back and gives in to me. "Who cares if we're late for a stupid little wedding?"

I've been eyeing the highway below us and haven't noticed a red Thunderbird full of crazy people, anywhere. "Wait, give me your phone, just in case," I say, and when I check the messages, the universe finally gives us a bonus. "Ha! Gram says they'll be twenty-five more minutes. They stopped at a rest stop." I toss the phone aside and continue driving my man crazy with desire.

"Gotta love those rest stops," he says, quickly pulling off my t-shirt, bra, and jeans and throwing them in the grass. We lie back down on our jackets.

"Mmm. Do you love this? And this? Shall I take a rest stop here?" I stop talking.

Gene groans.

A few exquisite moments later, Gene sits up and slowly rolls off my last piece of clothing, my thong. He gently massages my breasts, ass and calves with his hands, warming my entire body as he does so. After a few minutes, I playfully roll onto him.

"Do you think tourists in cars on the highway below can see us up here?" I kiss his neck.

"Too late now, isn't it?" he says, and pulls me in deeper. "They're getting the whole French experience!"

In a field of wild, fragrant lavender, we rock together as one, my body lowering and rising in unison with his. We find the perfect rhythm and soon become lost in each other's bodies.

I fall forward and start kissing and sucking his neck, lips, chest, nipples. After a moment, Gene takes me by the shoulders, looks me in the eyes, and rolls me over, moving his hands to my hips.

Arms spread out on the grass in front of me, I gasp for breath. The increasing levels of ecstasy are intense; I need to hit something, bite something. I need to call out! I grab at my jacket, take its sleeve, and stuff it in my mouth, biting at it to try to muffle my screams. It barely works.

When Gene calls my name, it sends shivers through me, washing a wave of release up my thighs, spine, breasts, neck. We fall face-first onto our jackets, spent.

Our breathing remains in unison as we bask in the afterglow. Gene turns his head sideways to kiss my eyebrows, one at a time. "Love you."

I kiss his lips slowly, softly.

"Love you too, but get dressed. We're going to be late for Gram's wedding!"

As he starts to slip on his leather jacket, his hand finds something inside his pocket. "Hang on, Petal. I forgot to show you this."

I'm scurrying to pull on my jeans and T-shirt. "What is it?" I grab the slightly crumpled photo that he hands me.

"It's our backyard garden. It's only just getting started. I totally need your help with it. But, I... well, take a closer look..."

I gasp. "It's the basil. Oh, our basil! It's grown so much! And the watermelon?"

"You should see them," he says. "Three of them are taking off. Told you that we had potential. We just had to get through the darkness."

"We've got potential," I look up at him. "I know we do."

"We sure do. If our last act was any indication." He clears his throat, then picks my panties up off the grass and shoves them inside his pocket.

"Oops, forgot those!" I say as I frantically pull on my boots.

"Hey, no worries, it will just make next time that much easier," he says, pulling me up to my feet with his right hand, and we head down the beaten path together.

Chapter Twenty-seven

May 5, 2017

11:07 p.m.

The gardens at the 17th-century Chateau Baumanière are breathtaking. Black Parisian-style patio tables sit under majestic mulberry trees, set with pristine white china for tomorrow's breakfast on the terrace. An olive grove and the fragrant formal gardens are down the cobblestone pathway to the right. I'm sitting in the moonlight at the edge of a gurgling water fountain in the chateau's charming country gardens.

When I read the brochure Gram handed me about this chateau, I nearly peed my pants. Seriously: Queen Elizabeth, crime-writer San Antonio, celebrities like Colin Firth, Hugh Grant, Bono, Pierre Arditi, and Johnny Depp have all stayed at this unique hideaway in Provence! I can't believe we got married here.

I place my white wedge heels beside me in the grass and dip my sore feet in the fountain, getting lost in blissful thoughts as I relive the last 24 hours in my mind.

It's our wedding night, and I don't think I've ever felt happier.

Mind you, this day hasn't been perfect. If things had gone off without a hitch, I'd be suspicious. I mean, this is me and Gene we're talking about. I'm a klutz, and he can be clueless about how anything works in this century. If there's anything I've learned in my four decades that's worthwhile remembering, it's that there is no such thing as perfect.

The hiccups weren't anything major. For one, I tripped over my wedge heels going down the pink rose-petal covered aisle in the formal gardens. Despite the weight of the crinoline in my gorgeous, but poufy, white and pastel pink strapless ball gown dress, I did manage to catch myself before falling, and we all laughed it off. Hallelujah, because the girls told me the dress is made of soft organza, which is part silk, over dolce satin. It's stunning.

Gene also thought it would be funny to feed me cake at our reception, but it turned into a messy food fight with everyone in the family, even good ol' Ostrich Minister Man, who, after marrying Gram and Eddie, traveled from Mornas with us to perform our wedding. I'm sure the hotel staff was none too happy about the mess we left in the outdoor tent, but what can you do when you've got a family like mine? I could smell sickly sweet icing under my nose for the last half of the night, which annoyed me profusely until Gene brought me a hot, soapy cloth, and a tall glass of bubbling champagne, with his apologies for getting carried away.

Right now, he's tucking Theo in (more like trying to get the three "kids" to calm down and get some sleep after such an eventful day) and changing into a t-shirt and jeans before joining me out here for a walk in the moonlight. I'm keeping the wedding dress on. I've never worn a more exquisite piece of clothing in my life. I'm wearing it until people tell me it's getting old! Or... maybe just until breakfast. Otherwise, I'll be wearing French toast down my cleavage. Hey, at least I know my own weaknesses.

Since it was such an intimate wedding, we decided to create our own vows on the spot, and later, Ostrich Minister Man went into the more formal ones. I wasn't nervous coming up with what to say to Gene. We've always been open and candid. I was afraid, however, that if I was going to speak naturally, I might say "crap," or "Fuckity," out loud, but Cici was right beside me, prepared to literally step on my toes if I let anything slip. I handed her my bouquet of white roses and pink, ruffled-paper-petaled sweet peas. We tied the bouquet up in the same pale yellow gossamer ribbon that had been wrapped around Gram's bouquet, as a symbol of how long we've waited for this day. The intoxicating scent of sweet peas and roses hung in the air as I spoke.

"Gene," I said, "I may not always like you, but I promise I'll always love you. I promise to help you raise Theo, and to help you get used to living like an ordinary man in this century."

Alyssa giggled at that part, but Jenna poked her in the ribs to stop her. My heart melted when I saw them acting like old times.

"I promise to be your friend and lover and confidante, in good times, and when the shit hits the fan. Oh crap. I didn't mean to say shit. Oh, Fuckity." I put my hand over my mouth. Cici forgot to step on my toes, she was laughing so hard. I think she was actually snorting a little.

"Katherine," Gene took both my hands in his and saved me any more embarrassment by starting his spontaneous vows, "I promise I'll always love you, even if at times I don't understand you. I promise to try to see things from your perspective, and to try to be fair and respectful when we argue, even if you insist on throwing pillows at my head or whacking me on my upper arm when you're ticked off." He grinned, and I bit my lower lip, hanging my head dramatically, in mock-shame. I do have to work on that temper of mine.

"With all that I have," he continued, "with all that I am, and for all intensive porpoises," he dead-panned, and I guffawed, with small tears of relief that my dating days are done, "I honor you."

"For all intensive porpoises, I honor you, too, love," I replied.

My heart rejoiced as we repeated our formal vows, and I heard Gene's teary, "I will." It moved me more than I expected. He leaned in to kiss away my tears, and I had to gently push him back, whispering, "Not yet!" because Ostrich Minister Man hadn't given him the official go-ahead to kiss me. Everyone laughed, Eddie a little louder than everyone else, and Gene's face turned beet red.

Soon enough, though, it was time for our first kiss as

husband and wife, and everyone cheered, hooting and hollering our names. Gene kissed me long and with passion, then lifted me up and swung me around gleefully. I'll never forget the sound and movement of my crinoline dress, how clear the bright blue sky looked, and the sense of inner peace that rushed over me.

"Hey, Princess, come here often?" Gene strolls up with a champagne glass in his left hand and sits down beside me at the fountain. He's back in his black leather jacket and jeans, but he's still wearing his rented black dress shoes. I guess he can't find his sneakers.

"I'd like to come here annually, if we can afford it." I clink glasses with him.

"Hey, you're the one who owns the business; you'll have to tell me how we're doing, Boss," he says with a smile and puts his right arm loosely around my back.

"It was an imperfect, chaotic, absolutely beautiful wedding day. Thanks, Gene." I hear myself sighing contentedly as I rest my head on his shoulder. If I were sitting on the couch, watching myself in the Bachelorette, I think I'd barf a little in my mouth at the gooey romance of this scene, and yet, it's really happening, and I deserve it. Everyone deserves their own fairytale ending. Especially the women who have battled and overcome self-esteem issues, depression, and abuse. Especially us.

"So, you want to take a moonlit walk through the gardens?" Gene asks, and I nod.

"You realize it's the luxurious honeymoon now," he says, "but in a few weeks, I can only offer you a moonlit walk through a watermelon garden. I hope that'll do."

I start to answer, but hear a noise and look back over my shoulder. Someone's coming up behind us.

"Sorry to interrupt, guys, but Gene was looking for these sneakers," Cici whispers in the darkness. I jump up and give her a big squeeze.

"Thanks for everything you did to make today happen, sis," Gene says to her as he starts to take off his dress shoes. It warms my heart to hear him call her that.

"So, you're a married man, now. I guess it's really over between us, huh, Genie of the Phone?" Cici says. "I should have enjoyed having you serve me more, while I could."

"It's over, yes. Only one woman is my master, now." He winks at me.

Cici hands Gene his white sneakers. He tosses them down on the grass, then uses one foot to squish down the heel on his right sneaker so he can place his left foot inside without bending down.

"What? What?" he says, seeing me studying his technique.

"Nothing. I just missed that so much." I smile at him. "I missed you."

May 12th, 2017

It was difficult to drive away from that charming Chateau on the hill after such a memorable week, but Gene promised we'd return to Provence someday soon. As long as we aren't heading there in a whirl of purple smoke, I'm all for it.

The trip to Avignon airport was uneventful, and I was

pleased we didn't have too long a wait in the lounge. Yes, lounge. First class lounge, to be exact. Gram splurged and sent us all home in first class suites!

We're in these private little sleep pods that let me lie back, nestled in with a thick blanket, and all the alcohol I want. I'm so excited and feel so blessed to be here instead of that cramped, stinky economy.

When the attendant hands me, not one, but two little bottles of Baileys, I lift one up and wave it madly over in Gene, Lyssa, Jenna, Theo, and Cici's direction. They wave back, but start spilling over with laughter. I've forgotten that the Baileys was unscrewed.

Shit. I've spilled the sickly sweet drink all over my face, boobs, hair, and the back of my freaking first class seat. The attendant rushes over with a towel to help me soak up the mess, but it hardly helps. He slowly leans over, sniffs my hair, and whispers in my ear, "Eau de Baileys?" He's right. I smell like some strange aphrodisiac perfume a bartender invented. I'm such a klutz!

Gene takes off his headphones, studies what I've done, and shrugs his shoulders. "Ask them if they have any more," he calls over with a smile and gives me a little wave.

It's bliss to be loved for exactly who you are.

June 2, 2017

Gram's new home is so luxurious, I may want to sleep over some nights, despite that Gene has built us a beautiful new home of our own.

It was Gram's idea to move into a deluxe room at Country Estates Retirement Home. She told me and Cici she was tired of trying to cook her own meals and clean her large place, so she and Eddie have moved into the penthouse suite, with all the bells and whistles you could imagine. They plan to travel to another home in France for six months of the year and have already bought their plane tickets.

We've come to visit Gram after my Zumba class. Gene convinced me to start teaching more classes, which I'd always wanted to do, and he's working on the expansion plans that got delayed. It turns out he's got a great mind for finances and marketing. He's going to need some work on his Zumba, though.

Once we get my business in better order, Gene is going to buy a restaurant down the street and revitalize it. He wants to call it Three Wishes.

As Gene and I walk by the party room hand in hand, I can hear speakers thumping and an odd clanging sound. What's going on?

We stand at the party room doors and study the scene inside for a moment, then turn and look at each other. Our grins are wider than the ones we wore on our wedding day.

Old people are shuffling around in front of the fire on the dance floor, beating pots and pans with sticks. Some are dancing with their walkers; others are dancing with their lovers. It's a beautiful sight.

Somebody spiked the punch bowl again, and I have a pretty good idea who it was.

Remarkably Great

More Books by Heather Grace Stewart:

Strangely, Incredibly Good

The Friends I've Never Met

Three Spaces

Carry On Dancing

Leap

Where the Butterflies Go

The Groovy Granny

Amazon Author Page: amazon.com/author/heathergracestewart

Want to learn more about Heather? Please visit her at:

Her official website: heathergracestewart.me

Blog: heathergracestewart.com

Twitter: @hgracestewart

Facebook Page: facebook.com/heathergracestewart

Thanks

I'm bound to forget someone, because so many people help me get a book from its beginning stages to the point where you're holding it in your hands.

First, thanks to Kayla and Bill for encouraging me to attempt a sequel to *Strangely, Incredibly Good*, as well as everyone at Morning Rain Publishing, the staff and fellow authors, and a few amazing readers who pretty much insisted I start the sequel, including Michelle B., Sarah, Patty, Steph, Elisa, Marcia & Mike, Lisa, Kat, Alexis, Melanie, Nadia, Deanna, Alison P., Alison B., Simon and Matt. Thanks to my editor, Jennifer Bogart, for her eagle eyes and friendship. I'd also like to thank my amazing 'beta readers' Julie, Brenda, Arianna, Nadia, Peter, Tracy, Jenn, Kenny, Bradley, Simon, and Christine. Thanks to my family and Bill's family for the unending support you have given me every year of my book-writing career, but especially this last one, as I toured and tried to reach new readers of *SIG*. You've all been so supportive, and have made the more challenging parts of this journey memorable. (Melanie and Nadia, will you ever forget building a wire-bathtub bookshelf in Mel's living room at midnight? I won't let you forget – it was crazy fun!)

Thanks to those I interacted with at Black Bond Books, Novel Idea, Chapters Pointe Claire, The QMJC, Queen's University's Ban Righ Centre, and everyone who reviewed *SIG* or passed it along to another reader. I appreciate every one of you.

What's next? Get a Ticket and hold on for the ride...it's going to be good. ;)

CPSIA information can be obtained at www.ICGtesting.com
Printed in the USA
LVOW06s1232050915

452967LV00033B/1136/P

9 780991 879533